Namaste Stories Volume 2

Matthew Treya

DEDICATION

To my wife and daughter. Namaste.

CONTENTS

ACKNOWLEDGMENTS

Thanks Anne Frid de Vries and Julie D

A GIRL HAS TO DO WHAT A GIRL HAS TO DO

"If they're innocent because they haven't really done anything, then you're innocent because you haven't really done anything." Gary Renard

"Good morning, class."Sean Lewis runs a corpulent, smooth index finger down a silken attendance roster, and all is well...

1

…until he lights on the "N's."

"Nascimento?"

He pauses and scans a sea of expectant faces.

"*Andrea* Nascimento?"

His voice is mannered, studied, his smell clean, showered, deodorized, but he feels a small tickle in his throat, like a prodromal cold sore on the lip.

"Aqui," one of the faces, short pinkish hair, pink glasses, pink notebook, pink Disney tee-shirt, blue jeans, leather sandals looks up.

"Eh-sorry. I mean 'here'," she apologizes.

"Welcome," Sean smiles, "From…?"

"Brazil," she says.

"Bem vindo," Sean forgets the "a" ending and slides his finger down to the next name, shrugging off a vague disquiet.

Sean studies the tops of the heads of twenty-two obedient students scratching away at twenty-two sheets of lined yellow legal paper when Andrea, pink pen in pink lips, looks up suddenly at the asbestos tiles and catches him staring.

She sizes him up, her face registering a fast flicker of jumbled emotions jumpier than an MTV video: curiosity, fear, hatred, pity, seduction, perhaps. And Sean hides the "OM" tattoo on his hand with his grade book and grins. He's relieved when she finally turns away and bends back over her writing, a look of—what?—disgust? Come hither?

He's not sure.

Can it be her? He wonders. *It was so dark. Her hair was not so short.*

"Bullcrap!" he finally mutters and turns away into the whiteboard.

But, he *knows* what she's writing—she's pressing hard, her pen is flying, the scratching audible—writing about a tiny shack in a favela high above the sparkle of a city. A dilapidated cab with a bad muffler and a soccer ball ornament dangling from the rear view idles outside. Aroma of feijoida filters through a beaded curtain, mixes with and almost makes tolerable his clean, nervous, antiseptic, *American* smell: spray starch, Right

3

Guard, Arm and Hammer, Dial, and Old Spice. An "OM" tattoo—so out of character—on a man's left hand. She doesn't understand his English, so can tune into it more keenly—dry, mannered, Carpenters and Cowsills, Ward and June Cleaver in separate twin beds. A soccer game from the radio crescendos-dimuendoes through the curtain, from the cab, and through the window along with jacaranda blossom. Dende oil and coconut on her chocolaty skin. Dueling Elvin Jones-polyrhythmic escolas de samba.

And then, for a brief moment, for the first time, his smells, his sounds, turn real, sweaty, animal-like, natural. Then cease. And, she's almost at ease.

Almost.

Sean pounds a fist on the white board, hoping that ridiculous hope that one's wife, one's daughter…is the one in five hundred, the miracle, the survivor thrown through the crack in the fuselage, thrown clear, the one that walks away with only cuts and scrapes, the one interviewed in People.

But then this…*Andrea Nascimento*…scrapes a final scratching flourish followed by an emphatic TAP! on her paper with her pen, scrapes her chair, corners her three pages and admires them. Satisfied, she sprinkles them on his desk.

My god! He smells coconut and dende oil wafting up from them. *She's written three pages.*

She puts hands on blue jean hips and waits while twenty-one other students drop their letters, too. *Don't leave yet*, he begs them all silently.

She juts her chin at the pile of papers.

He scoops it up, corners it, vertically, then horizontally, opens his attaché, eyes the open door.

"Ahem," she coughs, furrows eyebrows, juts chin again, and zeroes in on his "OM" tattoo.

He stalls, searching a *long* time for her paper.

She stares.

"I've been living in Los Angeles for three months," he begins reading her letter aloud as if reading his own death warrant. His eyes beg: *must I really go on?*

Yes, she nods, in no uncertain terms.

"Good," he says, "present perfect continuous, hee, hee." He looks over at a picture of Amy and the kids on his desk. "You could also use present perfect simple."

She taps her sandal on the tile floor.

Tap.

Tap.

Tap.

"Right," she says, "Obrigado." She laughs without smiling then stabs her chin at the pages for him to go on.

"I lived in the favelas above Rio," he pronounces it "Hee-o," "Not easy. A girl has to do what a girl has to do."

"Nice idiom," Sean says bracing himself against his desk.

"*Your* pronunciation is quite good," she returns the compliment, but still no smile.

Rio.

Stroke-able, reclining nude mountains

Yellow turbaned, glistening Bahianas squeeze papaya on Ipanema

Thongs undulate like the black-white sidewalk swirls

Gravity-defying capoeiras

Berimbaus

He bakes, coconut meat pale as his hotel towel, while in New York it's as cold and lifeless as the summit of Everest, concrete and steel everywhere.

A cabbie, his radio thumping samba,

Flings a pink perfumed flyer into the back.

"I'm no *tourist*," he tosses the pink flyer back. "I'm a *professor*. Latin-American-Studies."

"Well…then…perhaps in the interest of anthropological investigation, maestro?" The cabbie tosses it back.

And Sean nods, and the city lights shrink between the yellow pompoms jiggling in the back window.

And chickens squawk.

Dogs bark.

Mud and garbage.

A tiny shack with no sign and only a single candle flickering behind a pink curtain. And his, er, sociological research is *fulfilled* to the raucous cheering for Pele.

He pulls on his chinos and feels better piling the cruzeiros high on the pink pastel night table.

"Ahem," Andrea Nascimento coughs again. "Professor? Hello? Professor?"

"A girl has to do what a girl has to do." Startled, he re-reads where his index finger has remained. She laughs.

He read on, reads with the searching exactitude of a PhD student.

But it's not there, nothing, no mention at all.

He sniffs the paper, her. There's no mistaking? Dende oil. Coconut.

He sips coffee and twists his face.

"Every day," she begins speaking when he reaches the end, her voice and face softening, "everyday, I've prayed for you."

Sean spits out his coffee, spraying it on her pink tee-shirt and on his own blue button-down.

"Prayed you'd find... *Him*."

"*Him?*" Sean's afraid to ask.

"Do you know about... *Him*?" She hands Sean a tiny tract with a long, flowing hair, bearded white man on the cover then squeezes his hand over it, pats his fingers for good measure.

"Well…I…er…I…,"

She grabs his other hand, then squeezes both tightly, turns clamped eyes toward the ceiling, and an otherworldly language pours from her lips, pretty lips, almost orgasmic lips.

"It's gonna be a long, productive term," she says at long last, "it's going to be a nice LONG term."

"A LONG term, yes," he says, eyeing the door, "a VERY LONG term, indeed."

A STABLE OF MICKEYS

"Nothing real can be threatened. Nothing unreal exists." A Course in Miracles

It's moving too damned fast. This line, these red felt switchbacks, zig zags, as circuitous as a trail snaking up the Hindu Kush. It funnels a thousand restive moms and dads, kids with Mickey light-up pens and puffy, pastel Mickey autograph books. Funnels them like complacent cows to slaughter.

Too damned fast.

Impossibly fast.

Hanging video screens loop "Steamboat Willie", the air is stale, the light dim, but it's as obvious as this cavernous barn is big: it couldn't possibly be moving so quickly, unless…,

And, Sean grasps his daughter, Georgette's, tiny hand at the thought.

Soon, through a break in the throng, he confirms with a glimpse what he hopes is not true, and he squeezes her innocent hand tighter.

"Dad!" she complains.

Not one but two, two stylized, off kilter, kid's playhouse barn doors. And the line bifurcates like a slithery python's tongue.

"What an idiot!" Sean slaps his forehead. And instinctively he leaps—does an odd jig—interposes himself between Georgette and the two outlets.

"Dad?" she says.

"So, who've you got…so far?" he feigns interest in her puffy pink autograph book, peeling open a diagonally folded page then another, negotiating his way backwards and Rolodexing through a list of lame excuses for aborting the mission, but when he thinks of the hell he'll have to pay…,

He *could* just faint? Faint like he did at the World's Fair. Was it the August heat or those two ersatz ShakaZulus? Decked out in black-red feathered headdresses, white cowrie shell necklaces on shiny hard black chests, proud spears aloft in right hands, carved shields in left, grass skirts, wristlets, anklets.

But the shoes.

He cringes at the thought.

Exactly like his dad wore to the office: black lace oxford wingtips, and black knee socks.

A Japanese girl interrupts. Her costume is blue farmer overalls, straw hat, red bandana, straw in lips, and she flourishes them through the left door.

"*Door A*," she directs imperiously. "*Door A*, on the left, please."

13

Walt would turn in his grave, if he were really dead and not floating, his pencil mustachioed head at least, in that glowing crystal ball, a Medusa's head of electrodes hooked to the master computer in the bunker. He'd blow a fuse like the time he caught a Frontierland cowhand moseying through Tomorrowland. His disembodied head would do a Linda Blair in this bell jar.

For just to the right, in this unadorned service corridor—blatantly, shamefully, visible to all —the right branch of this human river of fidgety fathers and kids flows toward *Room B*. Some awful mistake, an illicit peek behind the scenes, off limits.

So, Sean maneuvers to Georgette's right side, hovers, enfolds her with his left arm, then steers her, peering over his own right shoulder as if on a gaining grizzly bear, steers her towards *Room A*.

"So, who you gonna get first?" he spreads open her autograph book, flips through some pastel pages, "Mickey? Ariel? Pocahantas? Snow White would go nice here." He pauses on a snowy page.

14

"Yeah dad, I guess." She tries to sneak a glance backward, but he intercalates his adrenalized body blocking *Room B* as if it were a blast of shrapnel, a hail of machine gun fire, an A bomb wave, a Chernobyl meltdown, as if she were a GI, a buddy in a foxhole. He sees the two ShakaZulus, right there on the *Room B* line, and shakes his head, two ShakaZulu kids holding lighted pens and puffy autograph books. All in grass skirts and colored headdresses.

And below the dried grass anklets? You guessed it! Black lace oxford brogues.

He positively clutches Georgette, and his salty tear falls on her shoulder.

"Dad?" she turns her blue eyes up toward him.

"It's okay honey," he summons a smile, and peering over his shoulder, edges her toward *Room A*. She rear-ends two kids in front of them.

"Where's the fire, buddy?" an angry dad glowers, "Plenty of Mickeys to go around," he adds.

15

"Exactly!" Sean mumbles, *"Exactly!"*

      Happy squeals emanate from *Door A* now just ahead.

"Almost there," Sean says, relieved but aware that like for a tight rope walker, this last meter, when your guard is down, is perilous. Anything can happen.

And

It

Does.

He hasn't even turned to check *Door B* one last time, when a child cries and in spite of his efforts,

Georgette

Looks

Over.

      A huge white glove engulfs the door frame of *Room B*, and a floppy black clown shoe the size of a small pizza flaps on the concrete. The shoe is topped by a red pant leg.

Tragedy is only averted by a quick thinking Vietnamese cast member in a pastel blue pants suit, who blocks the door with her arm.

Nearly averted, that is.

Georgette has seen it, and she looks away, then down at her autograph book, then to *Room A*, over to *Room B*.

Finally, she raises her eyes to her dad's.

Holds them on his,

And waits.

What can he do but nudge her the rest of the way, into *Room A*, where autograph books are held aloft like lighters at a Who concert, and Mickey is conclaving with the next lucky kid? A photographer records the scene for posterity.

"Georgette?" Mickey pantomimes.

"Georgette," Georgette responds, waving her red blinking pen. But her face and voice seem to say, "Duh, shouldn't you already know?" And she's not fawning over the larger than life scrawl, the exaggerated curlicue flourish underneath, the girlish supernova star dotting the "i".

Instead, she's examining Mickey with her tiny fingers right around the yellow bow tie. She comes close and sniffs, contemplates the ceiling. Her ingenuous fingers reach up to investigate a meshy sponge-like thing, a breathing screen, and a great white-gloved hand swats her hand away. Still, she probes with Johannes Kepler-Anton van Leeuwenhoek eyes trying to get the light just right.

"Okay, kid," a cast member in a pastel green suit nudges her on. "There's other kids on line. Say goodbye to Mickey."

"Bye Mickey," she says, and in turning, the light *does* hit just right, and she does a double take.

"Mickey!!" she yelps.

"Er, "Georgette, y'know that was Mickey's brother before," Sean is as jittery as if giving "the birds and the bees" speech. "Y'know? Brothers?"

But why is Georgette looking at him that way?

"Then her *brother* is a *girl* like this one?" Georgette inquires.

Instinctively, Sean looks at Mickey's feet for some clue.

Then, he and the pastel green cast member extend palms toward each other.

"Go ahead. *You* take it," they seem to say while Georgette cradles her puffy autograph book against her chest.

NORMAN'S LITTLE FIEFDOM

"Every individual as a person is a mask but fundamentally a mask of the godhead." Alan Watts

"*Sorry…no…more…electric…scooters!*" Norman slaps the sign on the counter and glowers at Sean and Marina, who's putting her foot down…well, *figuratively* putting her foot down, as it rests, never moving, on the metal footplate of her red wheelchair.

"An electric scooter," she demands, "or *nothing!*" She examines her withered body and the used car lot of *manual* wheelchairs,

20

then Norman's sign. Besides, she's just noticed Norman salaaming a white-haired lady into an *electric* chair.

"What gives?"

She's as livid as the Florida sky is infinitely azure.

She turns to her husband. "Sean, get me a goddamned *electric* chair," she barks, "now. N-O-W!" She wheels up to the counter, flicks handbrakes with fingerless black gloves, crosses her arms, Gandhi poising for his satyagraha salt march.

Sean steels himself then raises an index finger, but Norman disappears into a set of double red barn doors.

He reappears, a blur in a red *electric* scooter, which misses Marina by an angstrom, sets her blond hair aflutter; she pitches back just in time. He stares through her as he flits by, a gaze perfected over eons in this Siberian

21

Disney gulag, which most guests avoid, not in the TV commercials. Any more remote and they'd be behind the Wizard's curtain, the Potemkin village façade. No carousels, giddy kids, treacly churrascos here. It's Jiffy Lube, the cement—Gad!—*unpainted!*—smudged with wheelchair tire rubber like runway two-four at JFK.

What Norman says, goes. He's the law, the sheriff, the doorman with a hand on the red, felt rope. It's his domain, bailiwick, fiefdom.

"Go ahead, dear, tell him." Marina bangs her caster wheels into Sean's shins, a black and blue blotch peeking out from atop his white knee socks, then reverses, crashes again, like a determined icebreaker.

"Ouch!" He swats her away, a Doberman nipping at his ankles. "He's busy, dear." He points at the sign. "Can't you see?"

Norman salaams a purple-haired lady into his electric chair, a glistening new Caddy on the marble showroom floor.

"Thanks," he nods and stuffs a five into his golden habanero uniform shirt pocket, then busies himself behind the counter.

"Hey, what gives? Now!" Marina clips at Sean's heels like an angry cattle-driving mutt.

"Ahem, er, excuse me…,"

Norman, greasy wrench in hand, swagger stick, billy club, eyes him, a surgical nurse passing the wrong retractor.

"All's I have are these." Norman sweeps the junk yard of dilapidated chairs, *Property of Reedy Creek Geriatric Center* stenciled white on blue vinyl back rests, homeless-guy-in-hospital-bracelet-Fred Flintstoning-himself-along-the-Bowery-type wheelchairs.

"All out." Sean cocks a thumb at the chairs, mothballed Boeings, metal flapping in a baking Santa Ana wind. "Phew!" And he turns.

But Marina adjusts, tightens her folded arms, Martin Luther King Jr. at the wrong end of the Edmund Pettus Bridge.

"All out, he said. Let's go!" Sean tries to maneuver around her. "Damnit!"

Marina pops a front caster wheelie, two inches off the concrete, and Norman jack-in-the-boxes from behind his counter, greasy wrench in hand, uniform sweaty, a thin smile inchoate on his taut lips, a Sufi whirling dervish swoon transforming his face.

"Damnit! Let's go for crissake!" Sean's Travis Bickle in the mirror, *You talkin' to me? You talkin' to ME?* He grabs Marina's spongy handles, flips her brakes, yanks her chair around. Marina wriggles like a colicky baby.

"He's...,

All...,

Out!"

Norman grins. A beatific smile.

"Hey! You *too* buddy?"

He hoists an index finger at his compadre, his suddenly long-lost brother, his guru, his sensei. "Hey! Wait a sec, wouldya?"

He floats to the barn, a lover to the waiting arms of his beloved across a field of daffodils. When he re-emerges, he's piloting a shiny black electric scooter, its tires as immaculate as the soles of unworn shoes. He salaams Marina—the queen into her carriage—and cocks an ear to some faint sound.

"Why didn't you say so, sahib?" He claps Sean on the back. "Go on, get in." He offers Marina his hairy arm. "Go 'head." "Hey," he turns to Sean, "happy to oblige, especially with...," he cocks his thumb toward Marina. "Hey," he loses himself in the azure sky, "y'know what…it's on the house!" He seems puzzled as if coming to grips with some unfamiliar pleasure.

"But…?" Sean protests.

"fahgetaboutit," Norman rotates his palms like a carrier landing officer waving off an F-4. "Sahib, I said it's on the frickin' house, and I meant it."

And for the rest of the day Norman salaams as if in lunar gravity, steps to the rhythm of some distant carousel.

Sean, too, floats, a few lengths behind Marina, whose hair sprays like the mane of a galloping palomino. They've descended from a month on Everest, into the bustling spice markets of Kathmandu: Tibetan prayer bells, roasting kebabs, thangka paintings, ginger, yak butter. Guests part before her like a Red Sea.

"C'mon, hurry up." She pirouettes the black chair several times.

"Hey," Sean calls, "wait up. Y'know what that guy did? He…,"

But she bursts ahead.

And the camera pulls back, wide, and up, higher and higher. And there—quick, hurry, or you'll miss it—down in the corner of the screen,

Norman's little fiefdom

Bathed

In

A

Beam

Of

Radiant

Sunlight.

THE DO-GOODER

"...the selfish self...its love is assumed, pretensive,
and dutiful; its righteousness is hypocritical.
Its spiritual ideals are highbrow ways of inflating
the ego, and its beneficence has an odd way of
arousing resentment in its recipients."
Alan Watts.

A glassed-in guard buzzes Sean in, and he
crosses the dirty black and red-squared
linoleum day room, a sanctuary--if you
can call a grimy stained glass-windowed day room
with an anemic TV a sanctuary—to a bolted door,
tiny, frosted wire-mesh window.

He knocks.

No response.

Behind him, a plastic Wal-Mart Santa, a few strings of flashing lights on the wall, plastic pine sprays, an emaciated dusty plastic X-mas tree.

Rubber-thonged guys, stubble awash in flickering blue glow, encircle the old TV, devotees their pit.

Yellowed "Our Father" poster and a long roster of regulations haven't felt the warm caress of an eyeball in twenty years.

Why?

Why did I do this? Sean ponders.

Tendrils of cooking chicken—middle-school cafeteria, army mess, simmering in industrial-size pans, steamed trash cans—seep under the bolted door. Sean sniffs and dry heaves.

Why indeed!

Greg, that atrophied fixture on a filthy green blanket, cadaver skin, too long out-of-doors, the smell of too much fresh air, nights on crushed cardboard box mattresses, Thunderbird-pickled, once screamed at him,

"I don't need your fucking money!"

when he bent to stuff a crumpled five into Greg's stained Greek blue coffee cup. Screamed at him, an explosion of a scream that sent the decomposing coffee cup, its coins, the wire grocery cart, the bursting-at-the-seams plastic garbage bags, and Sean, too, all on their asses, onto the icy sidewalk.

"But...,"

"I SAID I DON'T NEED YOUR FUCKING MONEY!"

Electrons never stop spinning. Unthinkable. Against the laws of thermodynamics. Yet, a young woman in a business suit and yellow Nikes slowed, harrumphed, and

The crowd paused

And

Stared.

And another attaché, his face mano-a-mano with Greg's yellow, nicotined, spittle-coated beard, asked, "This guy botherin' you?"

"Yeah, gemme a cop; he's harrassin' me; I wanna file a lawsuit…,"

"I only wanted to…,"

"I know what you wanted to do, you…you… *do-gooder*…,"

"I just want to help's all…,"

"POLICE! HELP! POLICE!" Greg screamed.

"Bastard," Sean muttered, "ungrateful bastard!"

And the crowd circled,

Pulled its wagons in

"The Wild Ones"

"Do-gooder," one chanted.

"Lynch him,"

"Yeah, string 'im up," another picked it up.

"Get that do-gooder!"

"I…I…I…just…,"

And Sean was racing down Park Avenue South, the heat from their torches burning his neck, an angry posse

"To Kill a Mockingbird"

"Deliverance"

Yankel Rosenbaum.

He ducked down into the number six train station, jumped the turnstile, knelt behind a green dumpster, panting.

"Whew, that was a close on!"

But…

Apparently not close enough.

Will he ever learn?

The clunk of a deadbolt.

Big Wayne cracks the door.

Unsmiling Big Wayne, from yesterday.

Calls himself "Du-Wayne."

Woosh of stale chicken,

Service for two hundred,

Flows in.

Du-Wayne's massive torso, his huge forearms.

Huge forearms.

But wait.

Their black skin.

He recognizes it.

Funny.

Plastic-y, cadaver-like, too much time out-of-doors

Odor of nights-on-park-benches

Where has he seen it before?

Big Du-Wayne's black engineer boot makes a good door stop. Twenty smiley, red-tagged "hello my name is" volunteers hover—the server-to-guest ratio that of the QE2--try to get a glimpse, squeeze in to frame Big Du-Wayne like kids at a birthday party hogging the photo.

"I came to...," Sean fingers the red and white "hello my name is" on his breast.

"We don't need no help...,"

"Volunteer...,"

"We don't need no volunteers," Big Du-Wayne rolls his yellow eyes towards the glut of volunteers.

"But...?" Sean strokes his red and white tag, admires his concave reflection in a blue ornament on the Christmas tree, which coordinates smartly, indeed, with his red polo shirt. "But, you *hafta*," he taps the sticker on the word "hafta", "you *hafta* let me in...came all the...,"

"I don't *hafta* do nuthin'," Big Du-Wayne says, "I don't care you came all the way from China."

"Who the...?" Sean snatches his fingers back from the door just in time.

Slam!

"Goddamnit!" he yells at the door, "I'll sue you. You almost...,"

"Yo, what don't you understand 'bout we don't need no help?" Big Du-Wayne's muffled voice penetrates the door.

"Ungrateful bastard!" Sean shouts, bangs his white knuckled fist on the door, then storms toward the exit. The rubber-thonged TV guys look away from him, hold their breath when he nears, fixate on the TV. They've seen guys fly off the handle before; they *ain't* takin' no chances.

"Go 'head, someone say sompin'…go 'head," Sean shakes his fist.

They recoil then huddle-cower.

Sean pauses, muscles shivering like a race horse at the gate.

Taut springs.

Shoulders hunched, cocked triggers

Then

BANG!

He kicks a baby Jesus across the linoleum. It caroms around like an eight ball and comes to rest under a stained glass window bearing its namesake.

Thunderous tear of Velcro as he rips off his name tag, flings it at the glassed-in guard. The guard flinches, wards it off two-handed, then buzzes Sean out.

But, who can explain?

Tear of Velcro?

Buzz of door?

Hand still on the door handle,

the tingle of the buzz still in his fingers,

Sean smiles,

pulls, and

right there,

between dark and light,

his shoulders soften,

muscles un-tense.

"Says he doesn't need anybody?" he mutters to the guard who busies himself with a scrap of paper.

"Oh, yeah, guess he *really* doesn't need anyone...happens."

Sean's shoulders shift, then un-cock, re-seat
as if his osteopath has rammed both dislocated
humeri back into their scapulae with a dull snap.

Then he sees *the guy*:

A yellow-bearded guy

Any guy, really,

Spread out by the lake

Napping

His skin, *that* skin, when Sean gets closer, too
much time out of doors, scent of too much fresh
autumn air, dead leaves.

He pulls out a twenty and tucks it under his
filthy green blanket.

"Hell, "he says, securing it under the blanket,
"by the time he wakes up, I'll be miles away.

"Miles away."

FABIO

"The truth is there is nothing to find." Hyon Gak
Sunim

"You let it slam," I say. "Did not," he says. "In my face," I say.

"No way."

"Hmmmmmm."

We plop down across from the doctor, poker-faced, fingering Sean's chart.

Does no one else see him?

Not my husband, Sean, bald, reeking of refineries and mothballs, a hunched specter?

Not the good doctor, half-specs on his nose, afraid to look up from Sean's chart?

There!

Over there!

Leaning on the EKG. Cocky, like a drugstore cowboy.

Shhhhhhushhhhes me,

finger on lips, then saunters over, finger on *my* lips. Surely someone must see him, now? Or smell him, his oily chest, steaming coconut mango, his long blond hair silky straw.

But no.

Sean's eyes, reddened-grey, are on the good doctor, crinkling his chart. Sean's lips are moving: a silent prayer.

I brush Fabio away. "Go 'way," I whisper and squeeze Sean's cold, shriveled hand.

Sean turns. "What, honey?"

"Go away, uh, er, I mean I hope it's all *gone,* yeah, hope you're in remission. I really do."

But Fabio's not making it easy. Hands on his horse haunches hips, he pantomimes Sean. "Gimme this. Gimme that. Tea. No sugar. Can't drink sugar. D'jou wash these apples? Then he flexes his pecs like dueling bongos, pivots, and well, let's just say his red spandex hides nothing and… and I'm counting my nails, my French manicure, clicking, three? Four? I don't mean it really. I just can't help it. And Fabio's lips are counting along.

If I wear black for, let's see,

Five?

Six,

maybe seven?

Yeah, seven'll do it. Seven seems proper. Appropriate. Has a nice ring. Seven days and then…

And Fabio grins and shows his perfect teeth, and I grin back. He's close enough that his blond hair tickles my cheek, his strong hand on mine, captain cuddling co-pilot on the throttle.

"Cleared for take-off," he whispers.

"Cleared for take...," I whisper.

"What?" Sean turns.

"Mrs. Lewis...," the doctor taps the chart loudly, then again, "Mrs. Lewis, your husband...,"

"Oh my god!" I scream, "Abort," I whisper to Fabio. "Abort! Damnit! Abort!"

But Fabio pushes.

"Mrs. Lewis!"

"Abort, damnit!" I yank my hand away, and Fabio skulks over to the x-ray illuminator box and peers at Sean's film.

"Yes, doctor?" I smooth out my skirt, brush back my hair, sit erect.

"Mrs. Lewis...," The doctor's lips are moving. I can see them framed by a phalanx of diplomas on a wainscoted wall. He's smiling; Sean's smiling. He hands Sean a CAT scan, and Sean's flapping it, waving it like a West Point grad his hat, tossing it in the air.

"It's wonderful, honey," He hugs me, and I smell the New Jersey Turnpike on him. "Unbelievable!" he shouts, "A miracle!"

"Unbelievable, yes," I catch Fabio out of the corner of my eye, and he winks. "But…but…but I thought…,"

"Thought what, honey?"

"Well, I dunno. I just thought."

He cocks his head like a puzzled dog.

Sean's hand-shaking, slapping the doctor on the back, then arm around me, conducting me, dragging me, out the office, down the sterile corridor. I catch Fabio, tan face glowing in the illuminator box light, still studying Sean's x-ray, scratching his head, wiping a tear rolling out of his blue eye.

"I'm so-o-o-o-o sorry," I blurt out, breaking away from Sean, trying to face Fabio. "I…," Fabio reaches both powerful arms out to me, and I lift mine, and I take a step toward him when…when… a pretty young nurse in a tight pink uniform sings, "We'll see you in six months, Sean, uh, Mr. Lewis. We'll see you for the check-up in six months."

"Did she say 'Sean'?" I spin just in time to catch a wink fly between them, between Sean, my husband—I haven't seen him so tall, chest out, like the old days, shoulders back, face alive, his hand almost in hers, its trajectory broken when they spot me—between my husband and this nurse.

"Uh, yes, nurse, six months, I'll, uh, *we'll* see you in six months." He's grinning a goofy grin, *our* grin, which seems out of place here. It reflects in the nurse's green irises, and when he sees I've turned, he wipes the grin and stoops a bit. He flourishes the front door, bowing and scraping like the liveried doorman at the Plaza, and I thank him with great flourish myself.

"You're welcome," he exaggerates back.

"It really is wonderful," I say and catch Fabio leaning on the front desk chatting up the pretty nurse in the tight pink uniform.

WALL OF GURUS

"I just realized that I don't have to have an opinion about everything—what a relief." Dr. David R. Hawkins

"Guy oughta be grateful…on Thanksgiving." Al's looking at *me*, square in the face. He booms, ex-lawyer, ex-Marine, Great Santini. I almost expect a basketball bounce on my head.

I tug at my green tie, choking.

"…just once a year…not for me…for mom… and dad…," says Marina.

He's framed, crisp seersucker, by a half-circle blue Tiffany window—made it himself—Buddha on tangka, Botticelli's Venus on a scallop shell.

It's all delicious, turkey, stuffing, cranberry; delicious but at a cost.

"P.O.W.….Nam…Hanoi Hilton…stone cell… those damn guards." Al wags his finger at me, massages his eternally swollen jaw.

Then I crack, *too,* gagging, stripping off my green tie, blue suit jacket.

Bathroom mirror.

Hyperventilating.

Dry heaving.

Al's voice, Marina's crying, penetrate like the tapping code on the concrete cell walls.

"Never heard such a thing. *He* should appreciate his family. *You!*"

I tug-cradle my cheeks, pale and clammy. Jiggle-stretch the garroting tie knot.

"I'm sorry…it's not that I don't appreciate…," I conspicuously savor my mouthful of turkey-stuffing-cranberry.

"…appreciate!?…for god's sake…we were lucky if they threw us a rotten fish head on Tet."

"…Sometimes I just need a little time to…,"

Forks freeze in mid-transit, jaws drop, breathing ceases, a half-dozen pairs of in-law eyes like remora on my shark face.

"…I…just…uh…need time to contemplate."

Forks clang to plates like leg irons on concrete.

Snickers, eye rolls bounce around the linen table.

A clutch of interrogators smoking, laughing. What next? Bamboo shoots, electric prods?

"Contemplate…ha! Three and a half years *contemplating* my goddamn navel and the slimy walls of…I got yer contemplation, right heah!"

"Dad, please…," Marina shouts.

"He…," to Marina, then to me, "You…should be goddamned glad you *have* a little company. *I* am!"

"Dad, he's just a little shy…,"

"We're family for crissake," his bad teeth get in the way. "Nobody's gonna bite and…," He recoils from his daughter's hand. "Nonsense," he mutters, "Nonsense. Okay. Okay. He *does* drink, *doesn't* he?" He tilts a colossal Costco Chilean Cabernet, peaks eyebrows.

"No," I palm.

Still, he pours, a BMW cutting into traffic.

I push the bottle; he stiffens.

Wine sloshes, red stain spreads out over white linen, blue-white seersucker lapel.

"*Your* damn fault," he dabs wet napkin at lapel, table. Hand trembling, teeth gritting, bottle clanging against the glasses, he pours like an Indy pit crewman. "A toast, goddamnit," his glass tremors, raining red rain, "a toast!"

Two revving teenagers, candy-apple red-sparkle GTO's at a stop light.

He clinks and a tiny chip, a sliver, flies off.

Two charcoal-under-the-eyes quarterbacks, face guard clanking face guard.

Kennedy-Khrushchev.

Cuban missile crisis.

"Grrrrr…," he says,

"I

Said

A

Toast

Damnit!"

Rosanna's tray, a silver salver

A quiche

That free curried Hare Krishna vegetable feast

Washington Square Park

One summer

Long ago

The blue Tiffany scallop shell.

Turns the shade of the wall

In

That

Bookstore.

Sandalwood, patchouli, rose, peppermint,
musk, flutes, harps, tablas, sitars, Enya, deep pile
blue, track lights, muffled whispers, muted pastels,
blond wood, tarot card bag check, wicker basket
cowrie shells.

The inner sanctum

Fortress of solitude

Sanctum sanctorum

Holy of holies

Tubular bells

Music of the spheres

The wall of gurus

Altar

Wailing Wall

Racquetball wall high

Rainbow of book spines

Adi Da

Adi Granth

Chopra

Loori

Eknath

Gurdjieff

Krisnamurti

Govinda

Ramana Maharshi

Ram Dass

Vivekananda

Nisargadatta Maharaj

Nikhilananda

Farid Ud Din Attar

Yogananda

Ramesh Balsekar

Sai Baba

Suzuki

Watts

Wilber

Abstruse, exotic, quixotic, bogus, lunatic

Ives

Cage scores

Jackson Pollock pieces

Anthony Braxton song titles

Krebs cycle

Circuit diagrams

Mars base blueprints

Enneagrams

Holograms

Ordinates

Abscissae

Asymptotes as x approaches self with a capital
"S"

E, F, G, H, I, H

   or is it K?

Jiddhu Krishnamurti today, then. He's poised
on a soft chair: I'm on the low carpeted ledge.

Trane's "Love Supreme"

It's serpentine, raga, sheets of sound, playing in tongues, striving, tense, unfinished, becoming…

It's gonna be a long haul, hard work; I'll lay me down on a buckwheat hull zafu

Organic unbleached, hand-tufted cotton zabuton

Next week…L, Lama Govinda

M…Guru Maji.

But, his wine glass is an inch from my nose; bouquet erases sitar, sandalwood, I take a cowrie shell, turn in my tarot card, the door sign flips to

"Closed…Come Again."

"Happy Thanksgiv…," he's framed again by the blue-stained glass.

I throw back my head, down it in one gulp.

"…Thanksgiving," he finishes, "*now* we're talkin'," he beams.

"Say. That's okay. Can I get a little mo…?" I slice across half-way up my glass.

"Happy to oblige." His eyes open wide.

"Leave a little room for the swirl, the bouquet, right?"

"Right!" he says.

Soma?

Like soma wine!

Rig Veda.

Was that in the R's or the V's?

Can't quite conjure it up.

"Cheers," I say, "Al, cheers!" and we clink glasses.

And, no *need* to conjure it up.

MOTHER TERESA OF JAI ALAI

"No, I wouldn't touch a leper for a thousand pounds, yet I willingly cure him for the love of God." Mother Teresa

"Ooh," says the one in blue mechanic coveralls. "Ahh," say the other with a fresh crew cut. Blue

56

Coveralls has his pant leg up, and they're examining the pustules on his leg.

"They're givin' me this," Blue Coveralls lofts an orange medicine bottle, "itches like goddamned crazy," and he scratches to prove it. Crew Cut runs away, across a culvert, and under a desiccated tree.

I'm looking everywhere but at them. At my "Interior Castle," at the orangey flame that paints out a contrail. And the contrail stretches back down to the fronton, which shimmers out of a huge dry-lake-bed-cracked parking lot, like a pyramid out of the Sahara. At the threadbare grass, at the blue-white bus transfers the color of Mother Teresa's wimple.

And the orangey flame shrinks, then is gone.

Blue Coverall's minty ointment and a cloud of MD Twenty-Twenty precede him, then his tongue-flapping, tomato-sauce-splattered oxfords. When I look up, he's eyeing me through the bus shelter mesh, a convict at the visiting screen.

"Phew," he's close, but the screen's a molten ingot, "sure is hot."

Why I don't reseat my ear buds or study the Dollar Store flyers and ant hills, I'll never know.

"You ain't kiddin'," I say, and the contrail glints, stage three separating, on the verge of orbit, half way to the Azores. And his red eyes glint, too, on the verge of something himself.

Close up, he looks like Sanford, Fred G. Sanford, Fred, the old, stooped junkman with a ring of white beard Sanford, "I'm comin'-Elizabeth"-clutching-his-heart-Sanford. His hands, dorsal, are chocolaty brown, neither dry nor moist, cracked nor chapped, swollen nor shrunken, wrinkled nor smooth. Ventral, palms not calloused nor coddled. Nails not long nor short, yellow nor white, manicured nor bitten to the quick, filthy nor immaculate. His hands, had they protruded from a Brooks Brothers suit, a Rolex, had their fingers been gold-banded, could have clutched an iPhone, a silver Mont Blanc, a chrome stethoscope, scalpel, the maple neck of a Stradivarius.

Unremarkable, his hands, save for the frosted plastic hospital bracelet.

"Sure *is* hot," he repeats. "Say, I'm tryina' get me a little cash. You got forty cent? Git sompin't'eat."

"Maybe," I check my chinos but come up empty. "Sorry," and he waits till I go for my wallet.

"That'll do," he spots a few singles. "Got the chicken pops, itches like goddamned hell. This stuff doesn't do no goddamned good. Scratchin' all the goddamned time. Specially in this heat." He hoists his pant leg, revealing a moonscape of red sores, and I jump back.

"Uh, that's okay."

I hold out a buck at maximum extension, turn away slightly as if he's radioactive. But, he grimaces, bends, goes at his ankle with his right hand, the sound of two Wasa breads rubbing, a yellow road grader on gravel, his nails, little backhoes, scooping bloody debris.

"Thanks," and he reaches up.

And I hold the bill as if it's a tube of anthrax under a sterile hood.

"No problem," I say.

When I try to wriggle backwards, the burning metal mesh, a phone pole, and a newspaper machine block me in.

"Thanks," he comes toward me like Frankenstein, right hand raised in gratitude. To balk now would be to deny his very existence. We're a pas de deux, two lovers maneuvering for a kiss, our fingers inches apart and closing fast.

Nurse? Nurse! Glove please! Nurse?!

"Say, hey, you got a place to sleep?" I blurt out.

And

It

Works!

His right hand, my executioner's hovering over the switch, freezes.   And I'm mano-a-mano with his chapped lips, in his minty ethanol cloud.

"Sleep? Nah, need an f'in' *safe* place to sleep's fer shure. Maybe you could front me coupla more bucks."

Might be worth a few more singles to luxuriate in the safety of my wallet, stall for time. I dig in my pocket.

"Some guys sleep right there," he points at the dry culvert. The sores on his hand come within inches of my face, and I tuck in my chin as if from a waving, flaming torch.

Then...

Ahhhhhhhh....

The bus ...

Never more beautiful...

Rounds the corner...

Sky blue,

Clean as just-rained air.

Saved!

The driver's face glows welcome, the same face on the puffy Watchtower in the culvert. An air valve hisses, door swings open, whoosh of AC, antiseptic, starched, envelops us...the...chosen!

"Well, uh, sorry, my bus, guess I gotta be goin'."

"'Preciate it, anyway," he nods and continues where he left off, his hand a coiled rattler, a cat swaying its haunches, pre-pounce. The bus step a mere twelve inches, but, oh, what can happen in the last twelve inches.

Ask the Flying Wallendas.

An old lady with a surgical mask and a clear plastic Mickey Mouse change purse begins dropping pennies,

One at a time

One at a time

One at a time

Into the fare box.

Keep him busy,

Distract him.

Play for time.

The old triangulate-the-fix-on-the-ransom-caller trick.

The old get-the-suicide-hotline-talker-talking trick.

"Uh, say, you really should stay away from the juice," I say.

My rubber shoe on the rubber step, one hand on the chilly hand rail. The other on my pass.

A quick calculation.

Distance equals velocity times time plus one-half acceleration squared.

His right hand, arcing, inexorably, at this pace...

It

Should

Just

Graze

My outer cushion of air.

I'm gonna make it.

I've dodged the bullet.

I'm

Home

Fr…

"…but, I like it," he argues, and the driver's immaculate palm shoots up.

"Hold on," the driver slices down right after the old lady. "Gettin' off," he orders, "Stand back."

Beeps, hisses, and kneels; a wheelchair ramp unfolds like a castle moat bridge.

Sanford spins me by the shoulder, clamps his right hand on mine—a firm handshake.

"Thanks, man!"

One

Two

I count.

Three

Four

I hold my breath.

Five

"Your bus," he unclamps.

"My...bus."

Oh, pity the poor soul, unaware, reading his
sports section a millimeter from my virulent hand,
holding "Interior Castle" at arm's length.

Oh, the old woman with a wire shopping cart
whom I bowl over in the Winn-Dixie. How could
she know she's between desperate man and his
soap dispenser with a red cross logo?

I let the foamy balm marinate, scrub to the
elbows Ben Casey style.

My face.

My pen.

My glasses.

It's a wonder I don't strip down to my skivvies like the bums in the old East Side Airlines terminal.

"Interior Castle," lo, does not fare too well, and puffs up like the Watchtower. It goes into the trash.

Outside, the contrail, glowing pinkish, twisted, coiled like a broken Slinky, drifts north, still stretching…

All the way

To

Heaven.

HEY, HE WAVED AT ME

"I shape shift my consciousness into the heavenly realm of ever-expanding good." Michael Beckwith

The nerve! He pulls over…un-straps his harness…climbs down the stairs…his khaki uniform pants already have that eight-hour-behind-the-wheel wrinkle…comes around to the driver's side…reaches through… throws the lever…doors close…and the green stud

67

in his right ear flashes in the LED headlight, and he's gone.

A half-dozen of us eye each other like passengers on a doomed jet… *"Do you know what's going on?"*…then check watches and retreat into our newspapers.

I'll kill this little bald guy with the green earring, the Mr. Rogers black cardigan and grey goatee—if he comes back—I mustn't be late. I'll drive the damned thing if I have to.

"What say we commandeer…? I'm rallying the others—mutiny!—when the door hisses and he climbs the stairs.

"Okay," he sips unabashedly at an "I *heart* Yankees" cup, "Okay, let's go."

Clicks his harness.

That's it!?

"Let's go."

What cajones!

I'll have him fired! No. That's not good enough. Compensation for lost wages, suffering *and* hardship. No! Refund on my bus pass, and... and..., a free year pass. No! Free passes for all of us. No! A public apology from the CEO. No! He'll never work in this town again, not even the toy loco down at Disney.

"Dear sirs," I type at an imaginary monitor in the dark of the bus. But, it's not the bald, goatee-d face with the green ear stud and Mr. Rogers cardigan that inhabits my mirage screen.

It's Ronnie, grinning ear to ear, bright as the LED headlights on a Greyhound that's just heading down Broadway, white marble Lincoln Center its backdrop.

"Didja see it?" Ronnie's voice is the angelic alto in black and red satin robe of the New Canaan Pentecostal Church uptown, where a white, beardless, two-storey-tall Jesus presides. "It's a fourteen-dash-oh-six. 'S got forty-eight seats. Dash oh-eight's only got forty. Wow! Didja see it? He waved!" And Ronnie swoons as if the exhaust, cozy in this chilly October afternoon, is daffodils,

Shalimar. "Three-seventeen into Port Authority," he checks his watch.

"Yup, I saw it…look…gotta go…papers t'mark…see you tomorrow."

He tightens the knot on his skinny black tie with a fleet of little blue Greyhound buses in formation, strains under a backpack crammed with piles of Greyhound timetables, stacks of dog-eared letters. "Dear Ronnie, thank you for your interest in Greyhound…," scores of glossy centerfold fourteen-dash-oh-sixes, airbrushed, languishing, provocatively lit, waterfalls, seascapes, mountain ranges their backdrops. No school books here; he can barely decipher the letters. His white shirt, black slacks, tie *hang* there; his skin and kinky hair orangey-red—a young Malcolm X-Jehovah's Witness.

"Bye, Mr. P," he spits into yellowish palms, slicks back his short fro, ducks into the downtown Number One entrance. He lives uptown, but why go home? His mom's at her night shift, cleaning offices, his sister's with the baby. The Boeings hanging by fishing line from his bedroom ceiling, the same ones he salutes as they scrape the roof of his building on A Hundred-and-Thirty-Fifth, down the LaGuardia glide slope, only mock him when no one's there.

Downtown is Jerrisse, his "friend." "We do things together." His voice drops an octave when he says it.

Across the tracks, through girders, Ronnie disappears *up* the stairs. I'm still there when he descends again. But now he's Ron—"Call me Ron," he's been demanding lately, "Jerrisse calls me Ron." Ron is GQ preppie, penny loafers, argyle socks, tailored chinos, purple Izod. They all, too, *hang* on him. His tiny purple earring catches the light of an approaching Number One.

I don't have the heart to tell him. I'll write when we get to L.A. Invite him out. Good for an inner city kid, a little sun, a little fertilizer, for this wispy green shoot poking up through the crack in the sidewalk on A Hundred-and-Thirty-Fifth. Not to mention bus *nirvana:* seventy hours on a Greyhound.

The huge red circle with a white "1" on his train rounds the corner, and I remember Ronnie, uh Ron, in his Boy Scout uniform. Yes, yes, I know how it sounds; I'm not sure I'd believe it either.

But, I saw it!

An old lady, a cane, a wire grocery cart, red and white D'Agostino's bags. He proffers his Olive drab arm, leads her across Central Park West.

"Thank you, young man," she says.

"No problem, ma'am," he says.

The red circle, number one in the center, is a waning moon,

Full,

Waning gibbous,

Quarter,

Crescent,

New,

extinguished,

snuffed out.

I heard it maybe once, twice, the sound, in

New

York

City,

    very, very late or very, very early depending upon your proclivities, way up in the upper reaches of Central Park, above the reservoir, near where Ronnie, uh Ron, lived.

    Escape the hum, turn one's head just right, slow the bike, time it just right, 'tween the yellow cabs—or in a blanket of fresh snow…

The sound

The sweep, sweep, sweep

Brush, brush, brush

Eyelashes on a check

A lone pigeon cutting through the air.

Oh, not the flap, flap, flap of a flock of pigeons maneuvering for the stale bread from a homeless woman.

No.

But the soundless sound of a sail through the wind, a keel slicing through a still lake, a delicate eye brush raking, dusting over the softest powder.

Am I stretching the reader's credibility beyond the breaking point?

It's a sound one *feels* more than hears.

It's the sound of mown grass.

The manila envelope came with that sound, an LA version, a glossy of Ronnie, uh, Ron, in Boy Scout uniform grinning the grin of "Hey, the bus driver just waved at me, *me*!", and

Beneath him

The years

1972

To

2003

"Ron," the note is hand-written--Jerrisse is the only one who called him Ron--"Ron was comfortable at the end. He asked me to tell you everything was okay. It spread rapidly. It was over quickly."

Do you doubt me, dear reader, for...a third time?..., yet when the bus stops, and I walk forward in the dark—the letter, "Dear sirs, why don't your goddamned drivers...?" revolving in my fevered brain, the bald driver with the goatee, the green stud, the Mr. Rogers cardigan, sidetracks me, blindsides me.

"Have a good day," he says, voice octaves higher. "Look, sorry about the stop back there, just doin' another driver a favor's all."

His skin--is it the light?—has taken on a decidedly red-orange tint.

"Transfer?" he turns.

He's grinning a "Hey, the driver waved at me" smile. And was he wearing that tie with the fleet of blue Greyhound buses in formation when I climbed on?

With yellowed palms, he spit-palms his bald head as if he has a full head of kinky red-orange hair.

"Have a good one," he says.

And the blue number on the back of the bus recedes, disappears around the corner, a waning moon behind a bank of clouds.

SAINT FRANCIS OF THE BARCALOUNGER

"While you are proclaiming peace with your lips, be careful to have it even more fully in your heart."
Saint Francis of Assisi

F rank Faulkner's popcorn is the ecstatic nectar in the throat of Saint Theresa of Avila. He's tight and wiry, perhaps *too* tight and wiry, like a middle-aged marathoner who's put in too many kilos. He's the image of his hero, Francesco Bernardone, down to the strange bowl haircut, that immanent tonsure, but sans the beard and twice his age, three-hundred-dollar Nikes in lieu of Francesco's sandals.

Right now, Frank's higher than Francesco Bernardone, who's teetering on a terra cotta roof, arms outstretched, Christ-like, sneaking up to rescue a lost baby sparrow on the huge plasma screen TV.

Francesco Bernardone loses his balance; Assisi, brown and hilly and the perfect blue sky wobble— vertigo

> Blue
>
> Brown
>
> Blue
>
> Brown
>
> Like a tumbling artificial horizon,
>
> The crowd gasps,
>
> His blue robe catches under sandaled feet

But he scoops up the sparrow, regains his balance, then, holding the little bird trophy-like, grins through beard and…

The crowd applauds.

Frank *is* Francesco; his bottled water *is* soma wine, his popcorn…

But then, a cloud passes over this perfect Assisi blue sky.

Claire, his just-teen daughter, admits a mote of light, which washes out the TV.

"Hey, dad?" she screams above Lady Gaga on her iPod," what the f' is this rated?" She—in pink shorts, just short of Gaga's Lucite bubble dress--with her pink fingernails, indicates Francesco, who's just dropped his robe around his naked ass.

"Now I can see!" Francesco is exclaiming; Frank, eyes teary, parrots him, "Now…I…can…see!"

But the moment is ruined.

"Close the damned door," he lashes out.

Is he angry at Claire because she's more "Gaga" than she is her namesake, Clare, or because *he* can't quite summon up that original ecstasy, like an alcoholic chasing the first buzz? Because he's somehow a changed man?

Still, he persists.

"This is the scene. This is the scene!" He ignores his daughter.

And Claire him, instead fiddling with her iPod, with a stack of blu-rays.

"Mom said I could finish it," she waves "Home Alone" in his face, "Great film, dad!"

"This scene…," he fans her away, backhanded. "I'm tryin' t'…,"

"'Home Alone' dad. Y'seen it?"

"This's the scene where he walks away forever," he shushes her, "brings chills, so beautiful," he mock shivers.

But Claire steps in front of the TV, eclipsing Francesco.

"Dad! Dad! Mom said!"

And Frank's trapped in a stall-spin, on an "A" express watching his local stop, Seventy-Ninth Street, fly by, watching a lover walk away—but wondering, too, perhaps, *what did I ever see in her?*

And, Claire pops Francesco Bernardone out and Kevin McCallister in; the yellow, brown, ochre hills, the pinkish white stone of Thirteenth Century Assisi give way to the verdant palms, Eucalyptus, papaya, flowering pink-red hibiscus, the immaculate, irrigated lawns, the SUVs of Twenty-First Century L.A.

"No damned fair," Frank complains.

"Mom said…," she ups the volume, plops down next to her dad on the Barcalounger.

"Mmmmmm…," she scoops out a fistful of *his* popcorn.

He lunges at the blu-ray, yanks out "Home Alone" and flings it to the bamboo floor.

"Mommy said…," she retrieves the disc.

"*Daddy* said...," They scuffle over it.

In.

Out.

In again.

Out again.

"No fair."

"Is, too."

It's a two-man saw in a lumberjack contest.

A standoff.

"Isn't."

"Is, too."

He's in a graveyard spiral. If he can't get these pedals, this throttle, the yoke, working in a second, those red tile roofs, aqua swimming pools, black SUV roofs, green palms, spinning and zooming in...

"What's going on in there? I can't handle *two* kids," his wife, Marina, looks up from a mound of sliced tomatoes in the kitchen, dabs hands on a red and white checked gingham apron.

"Uh, nuthin'."

"Nuthin'."

Claire has *her* disc in and playing and *his* secreted under the couch pillow faster than a three-card Monte dealer.

"Where is it? If I find it, I…," he's on hands and knees, huge black flashlight.

Claire's stuffing more of *his* popcorn, laughing at the screen.

"*This* part," she mimics him, "this part, in the church, ya gotta see it!"

"Where'd you hide it?" still on hands and knees, wielding the long flashlight,

Wielding it now

Like a club

"why, I oughta…,"

"Oughta what?" Marina is between them, blotting tomato-y hands on apron. "I'll pull the goddamned plug…,"

"*Here* it is!" he pumps his blue-ray like a Stanley Cup, then Francesco is amidst the grey-white stones of a half-built church in a hilly green, wild-flowered meadow, yellows, purples, blues, sparrows flitting, bees buzzing, butterflies fanning.

But not for long.

Marina yanks it out, clucks her tongue.

"How

Could

You?

Saint Francis, my ass, pardon my French, indeed. You only wish!

Now

let

Claire

watch!"

"Okay, but I think the Tupperware needs sorting," and as he's getting up from the floor, Marina slams him into the couch so hard that he bounces back up a foot.

"Not so damned fast!"

"The laundry?"

"Fire 'er up," she tosses Claire the remote.

"Oh, I get it, 'Clockwork Orange'," he spreads both eyeballs wide with thumb and forefinger.

"Turn up the volume, Claire, dear," Marina says.

Frank's eyes *see* the little blond kid, but in his brain, Pope Alec Guinness dismisses Francesco Bernardone in a brown robe and rope belt. Frank tries to summon up tears as Francesco genuflects, kisses Father Guinness' feet. He readies himself for the remembered bliss, the expected bliss, the rush, turns his eyes inward.

"What do you want, my son?" the Pope asks.

"I want…

What…

What…

What…

He…

Wants," Francesco answers, and Frank's lips move.

What *He* wants.

Frank waits.

But where's the swoon?

Nothing.

The Pope, the Pope himself, kissing Francisco's filthy feet?

No greater scene has there ever been.

But *Saint Francis, my ass* rings in Frank's ears.

Saint Francis, my ass.

And then, he hears a choir, a celestial pipe organ. Smells the incense.

Is this it?

Ah, the rapture.

But the church, the choir

Are on the big screen plasma.

An old man

A lonely old man

In a church pew

Looks up to a choir loft above the organ at his estranged daughter, eyes heavenward, singing.

The little blond kid, Kevin, terrified of the old man, watches him watching his daughter.

And Kevin looks back at the old man the way Francesco was *supposed* to, the way Frank remembered.

"I wish I could speak to my daughter," the old man, avoiding the choir loft, confides to the kid.

"Why don't you?"

"She probably won't want to speak to me."

"How'll you know unless you try?" Kevin asks. "Whataya got to lose?"

The old man looks sidelong up at the loft.

"Maybe I will," he says.

"Yeah, you should."

And Frank's eyes well up.

What's going on?

What the hell *is* this?

This is the wrong movie; this isn't supposed to…,

And his daughter, Claire's, sneering, Lady Gaga poker face softens as she watches her dad. Just for a nano-second, the gasp between iPod tracks, there's a hint in her eyes of Sister Clare's blue eyes when they meet Francesco's across the half-built church in the meadow of yellows, purples, blues, and reds.

TAT TVAM ASI

"…a part of us is in the Himalayas…a part of us is in the roses…" Bhagwan Rajneesh

Damnit! Here, too? Doggin' me to the ends of the Earth. Antarctica. Even here?

Mary in a slice of French toast, a poodle's fur.

Christ in a tortilla, a turtle shell.

Joseph in a wet spackle spot, a tarnished teaspoon.

Here? Mom's face?

Eyes forever closed, before their time, and bulging with horror beneath.

Her face in bluish-white Mount Erebus as the jet banks left, lines up with an oil-barrels-on-snow runway.

I try.

Grind my boot into the ersatz runway,

Shake my blue balaclava

My green furry hood

Breathe frigid vapor cloud huff of breath

Clockwork-Orange-stretch my eyelids

Turn away

Turn back

"Oh, look!"

Feign startle

Carve a huge "7" in the snow,

iTouch-at-arm's-length of myself setting foot on my *seventh* continent.

Scott, Byrd, Amundsen, Shackleton.

Still, Mom's Erebus bluish face, her green eyes, even *under* sealed lids, follow me like Uncle Sam's in a post office.

Wherever I go, there I am.

It's no use.

Seven *continents*, all seven, and she, her face screwed up in pain, has followed me to each and every one as if *I* might explain to *her* what my father did.

Swirled blueberry sundae sky.

Waltz of snowflakes

Tip of the glacier, blowing snow…

"Reminds me of Everest," Niki, a short, wiry, blond Australian woman in a powder blue parka says.

"You *climbed* Everest?"

"Climbed the seven highest on all seven continents."

"Oh?" I ram my iTouch deep into my parka pocket. "All seven *peaks*!"

"Funny thing about Everest, though," she arcs her glove, "I'm up there, death zone," her voice lowers, reverential, "filming, sticking flags, posing, y'know…look over to Changtse…, and like Christ in a cracked windshield, I see *him* plain as day, *Tim*, that bastard, giving me the heave-ho. *That's* never in the brochures. Must be the oh-two?" She palms her forehead, then cups an invisible mask over her mouth and sucks in a deep breath. "Not fair, really."

"Wow, I thought it was only me," I say. "My mom. I was thirteen…,"

"No, no…each one…every time…and always the summit," Niki says, shrugging her puffy blue parka and looking off into the distance. "My Sherpa, Norbu, would look, kneel, point. 'Lha,' he would say, voice so gentle, 'Lha'."

"'Norbu, don't be ridiculous. That's just Tim, the bastard,' I'd say and, I'd fan them both away. 'Lha,' he'd insist, backing off, bowing, pushing that thick black shock of hair off his forehead."

"Ridiculous," she turns to me, turns palms upward. "Occupational hazard, I 'spose."

"Yeah, no kiddin'. My mom. I was thirteen, uh…," but she's half-way to the Sno-Cat.

The Sno-Cat rattles us like frozen bait in a pickup bed, denies speech. Niki's in front, staring at her Tim-in-Erebus; I'm in back, following my Mom-in-Erebus through the frosted window.

Snow's flying.

Wipers going a mile-a-minute, in synch

both right, like a lineman marshaling an Airbus with two orange wands. Both indicating me in back.

then both left, Erebus in the far distance, drawing my gaze out to infinity.

Me, infinity, me, infinity

A, B, A, B

Flap, flap, flap, flap

Some lunatic parakeet

But I don't get it.

And then

Imperceptibly

a smidgen, a degree or two, with each arc of the blade

They drop out of phase

It's hard to pinpoint

When does day become night?

concave become convex?

Now

Meeting in the middle, at Niki, in the front,
lingering.

Then one right, to me in back.

Other left, to Erebus, to infinity.

Sound changes.

Thwack

Thwock

Thwack

Thwock

And, Mrs. Kershaw, yes, Mrs. Gladys Kershaw,
my eighth grade Algebra teacher, a hunch-backed
woman with a leathery face and rusty-skates-on-a-
blackboard—her blackboard—voice, grey hair
pulled back in tight bun, a dead ringer for Dersu

Uzala or maybe a Nepalese Gorkha grandma with way too much time on the harsh plains, is wagging an arthritic index finger at the board.

Then at me, explaining.

"You are Niki," she screeches. "A equals C."

Then at Erebus

"And Nicky is Erebus. "C equals B."

I stare blankly.

"Don't you see," she's squealing now, cackling. She points again at the board. She's written it. "Ergo. Quod Erat Demonstratum. If A=C and C=B. Principium Transitivus. Well, then...,"

"A=B," I beat her to the punch.

"Good," she says.

"You mean I am...?"

"Precisely," she says. Then addressing the class, "Now open your books to page seventy-nine and do one through eighty-five, odd."

"Oh c'mon Mrs. Kershaw, all of 'em?"

"All of them," she says, "You'll thank me some day."

"*Erebus…and…*," I finish to myself and start factoring number one.

Back at camp, there's an oil spot in the snow; a little shrine has been erected, roped off by sticks and yellow tape, like some tortoise nest about to hatch in the sand.

"They say that's the Virgin Mary in there," Niki points, tries to limn it out. "Looks like a damned oil spot to me. Let's get some coffee. I'm freezing," she turns, tromps away angrily as if she's seen something else, too.

I crunch around it, then fall to my knees, reach close with my glove, cock my head this way and that, then try it again from another angle.

Nothing…not even Mom.

After coffee, I come back. It's a different light, but...

Still, no luck.

I glance over at Erebus. It's quite beautiful, a snaking wisp of vapor bathed in midnight sun, and the infinite sky shimmering greenish-pink Aurora Australis.

Quite beautiful, indeed, says Norbu from somewhere, or is it Mrs. Kershaw? Hard to tell. The voice is a cross between kneeling in powder snow and dragging too-long fingernails across a chalky equation-filled blackboard.

PLEASE CALL AGAIN

"If anyone wants more dollar bills, he must do his multiplying in the Invisible."

Joel S. Goldsmith

Reverend Clark Burghee holds head in hands, massages his temples. It's a cozy office, a warm red rug. Dark wainscoted walls. The odor of Middleton's cherry blend.

"The sins of the flesh," he writes in a long, yellow legal pad, then crumples and tosses it across the room. Two points! Into the corner wastebasket, a toy basketball hoop on top, a gift from his daughter.

"The wiles of the flesh," he writes. No. Crumples, tosses, massages his head.

"The troubles…," crumple, toss.

Down to the last yellow sheet.

"Problems…," he writes then scratches this out, too.

"Temptations…," write, scratch.

"Evils," write, scratch.

"Evils," he writes it again, slides his chair back, strokes his goatee, circles the word.

"Evils."

"Evils of the flesh," he writes out, makes four 3-D exclamation points with shadows.

"The Evils of the Flesh," he writes it again, adds a half dozen underscores, four stars, one lightning bolt.

Then, after all that, he shakes his head, scratches it all out, crumples it, tosses it, and massages his temples.

"Thirty grand," he prays to a wall of austere, mustachioed former reverends staring down at him from the wainscoting. "Thirty grand is a lot of cash. What the hell am I going to do?"

He fills his pipe, lights it, and exhales a large cloud of Middleton's Cherry Blend.

"What should I do?" he appeals to Reverend Bean, the kindliest of a stern-looking bunch, in a plain white shirt, black waistcoat, under-the-chin well-manicured beard, clean upper lip.

Then, Reverend Bean's dark eyes on him like a surveillance camera, he plods over to his heavy oaken bookcase, peels out a gold-leaved, red morocco "Robertson's Sermons," continues over to his Winston Churchill stand-up desk at the window, and pretends to read.

But…

It's the little pink-signed lingerie shop, Ludivine's, on the corner of Second Avenue he's, uh, *reading*. The shop window, bathed in the very shadow of his church steeple glimmers, white hot spots on purple, red, white, and black

Things...

Articles...

In the window.

Is it the Pavlovian tinkle of the little shop doorbell or the aroma of kasha varnishkes and palaak paneer that causes him to salivate? Is that Ludivine herself flitting by in her slinky red spangled dress?

From the pulpit, when Clark slides his Ark-sized Bible a tad to the left, Ludivine's red skirt ignites the second seat, third red-cushioned pew, right, and he leans on the Bible to prop himself up and keep his index finger glued to his spot in the homily notes.

Thirty grand? By the end of the month?

He strokes his goatee twice, savors his reflection in the window.

Thirty grand? Or find a new church? It's no use. I barely make that in two years!

"I

Must

Needs

Do

It!"

He slams Robertson shut and makes for his desk like an ice-breaker full steam ahead through a thick sheet of ice, heads for the *white* legal pad betwixt the Sunyata-blank yellow pad on the right and Marina and the kids in an unstained wooden frame on the left.

The white pad summons him like the Sirens. He takes it in his trembling hands, and it conjures up Ludivine and her blazing carny-lit shop window.

"Whew," he tents his black minister's shirt, letting off some steam and drops the pad like a vial of swine flu.

The yellow pad.

The tendons in Marina's neck nearly bursting.

Reverend Bean.

He's paralyzed.

Then he yanks open the left bottom drawer and stows the photo and the yellow pad under a Bible and slams the drawer shut.

"I must needs do this. The wife abideth…," he gets up, flips the dusty portraits one by one, pausing at Reverend Bean.

Does he actually wink? Does he really say, "Clark, three thousand dollars doth not groweth on trees?"

We shall never know, and Reverend Clark flips him over, too, nonetheless.

Clutching the white pad, he races over to his stand-up desk, which he shifts until it's just right.

He re-lights his pipe, lets out a great cloud of cherry blend.

Ludivine…, he writes, but then stops dead in his tracks. He stares at the pen—a gold Cross, a gift from Marina—like it's a scorpion.

"Yikes!" He flings it to the red rug.

He runs to his desk, rummages through a drawer like a crack addict and finds the cheap pink pen, the very pink of the shop sign.

Ludivine…, he re-writes, holds the pad at arm's length, turns it this way and that, smiles, and then it's off to the races.

He can't *not* write.

This pink pen flies as if the Devil himself is channeling. And, the study fills with cherry smoke.

Ludivine, a tigress in slinky red skirt…the sanctuary empties, the muffled stab of her red high heels in the red carpet…their eyes meet…the delicious Reverend Bean…a fine specimen of a man…in a Richard Chamberlain-Thorn Birds kind of way…

"Whoo-ey!" Clark cries out, flapping his wrist and fingers, rattling the portraits on the wainscoting, "whoo-ey!" He tents his black shirt again, licks his lips, sucks on his pipe, presses the pink pen so hard it nearly flies apart, his words carving furrows in the white paper, page after page after page like cheap movie calendar pages.

"Gee," he laughs and sees himself floating in a blue pineapple-tiled pool on Maui, Marina in huge Jackie O. shades under the green umbrella with a stack of cruise brochures and a tiny yellow umbrella in her Margarita, "How'll we spend all the money?"

"I hath waited so long," sayeth Reverend Bean, Ludivine cradled in his muscular arms.

"Lo, I've greatly longeth for thou," she uttereth, limp in his embrace.

Clark gulps down one paper cone shot from the water cooler after another, then runs back to the stand-up desk. Poor, sad Clark, poor Reverend Clark, in his writing frenzy, his artistic transport, this pinnacle of creativity, this hollow bamboo flute conduit for God; Tolstoy himself would have killed to achieve *this* state,

Yet completely oblivious,

Oblivious but ecstatic

Happy…

For now, anyway.

Anon, her red frock fluttereth to the red carpet whilst he unbuttoneth his white collar...his black trousers...,

But, hark!

Do ministers' black trousers *have* buttons? Who's to say? In Clark's fevered, deluded, naïve Quaker mind, they do, an whole slew of them.

"Les boutons! For god's sake, Clark, tu est fou. Buttons?" Ludivine cackles in the perfume-y pink-walled back room of her shop.

Clark, sipping an egg cream, hangs on her every nuance.

"What? Too racy?" he enquires, still in the dark.

The smell of kasha wafting in from next door is making him ravenous.

Then Ludivine's pretty face screws up as if she's bitten into a fiery morsel of chicken vindaloo.

"Gar-tairs? He's wearing garters? Ziss takes ze cake!"

"For his knee socks," Clark explains.

"…her unadorn-ed eyes, like the plain, white-wash-ed barn walls?" Ludivine takes another bite of vindaloo.

"What?" Clark sips his egg cream.

"…his loins burn-eth like the fires of hell… qu'est que c'est la?" She flops the pad closed, and delicate hand on the shoulder of his black shirt, edges him out the front door, flipping the sign behind him. "Sacre bleu," she mutters, "Mon dieu."

"Please call again."

"We could kidnap...uh...*dog*nap...Dr. Lerch's Maltese. No one'll ever suspect." Clark suggests, and Marina drops his favorite blue Pendle Hill mug in their tiny kitchen just down Seventh Street from the church and the pink shop. "He'll pay $30,000. Twice over. No harm done. Whaddya think?"

"You're not serious, right?" Marina says, sweeping up a dozen stained shards of coffee cup from the yellow linoleum.

"Does *this* look like I'm kidding?" He hands her a carefully folded piece of used white legal paper with something pasted on the other side.

"D-O-C-T-O-R L-E-R-C-H," says the hodge-podge of individually cut out magazine letters, "I-F

Y-O-U W-A-N-T T-O S-E-E B-I-N-G-O A-G-A-I-N…,"

THE SPOILED BRAT

"The time to live is now...the time for now is live.
They're gonna pour you through a great big sieve.
Give all the love you can give."
Buzzy Linhart

A pile of clean, warm white bath towels in Casper's arms all but blocks his view of his wife, Melissa.

"This guy," Melissa peers over the top of her crossword, "Honey, you should see this guy. Sits around all day, tanning his beautiful body, in a lounge chair. Luz waits on him hand and foot.

You like a beer? Can I fluff your pillow? Like a massage? You look stressed. What a baby, what a goddamned spoiled baby, a real sugar mama. Just 'cause he's ten years younger doesn't give him the right…,"

"Must be awfully good in bed," Casper interrupts, "real stud or…uh…?"

"Hung," Melissa saves him the trouble.

"Well, you said it…I wasn't gonna say it that way, but…,"

"How else t'explain it?" Melissa sips her chamomile tea.

"What's he do?"

"Works on his goddamned tan," Melissa says.

"No, really, what…,"

"Some kinda business; *she* really brings home the bacon. Makes double what he does."

"Porno star?" Casper says.

"I wasn't gonna say it. Nah, little old for that," Melissa says. "But…I wouldn't throw him outta bed," she looks up at the ceiling then pats Casper's belly.

"Nice six pack," she says, "Nice eyes. A deep blue," she laughs.

Casper looks at his bare feet, at the place where his low socks end. The line, the demarcation—between alabaster feet and his nicely toasted ankles seems particularly pronounced, reminds him of where the black Rio Negro meets the white Solimoes. He reaches down to massage them.

"Oh!" Casper says.

"What?" Melissa says.

"Oh," he repeats.

"Right," she says. Her faraway eyes look faceted, like the compound eyes of a Drosophila, but in just six distinct glistening sections, like, well, like *his* perfectly cut six pack.

"Hunh?" Casper fondles his convex gut.

"Well, honey, at least *you're* not like that. That's why I married you." Her six eye segments re-merge into one, one oddly distended, globular, bulging, and glaucomic, it's glistening sheen displaced by a cloudy-overcast at once content and disappointed.

Caper unloads the dishwasher, stacking plates, cups, glasses, pots, lids, forks, knives, and spoons high and low, opening and closing drawers, slamming cabinet doors. Melissa grimaces and sticks her index fingers into her ears.

"*You* wouldn't be like *that*," she announces. "You wouldn't be like *that!* Luz works like a dog, a real Chinese amah, guess it's her Filipina blood. How else t'explain it? Does everything: cooks, cleans, shops, washes, comes home after a full day at work, sometimes OT, ten, twelve-hour days and…and…and…hand 'n foot…," Melissa splutters. "He expects *her* to fix a meal, from scratch, won't eat it if it's not from scratch, no cans, microwaves, he pats his six pack, *my physique, honey, gotta watch what I eat,* no processed, no trans fats, lo-carb, high protein. For god sake!" Melissa sighs.

"Sheesh," Casper agrees, "*She's* gotta serve *him?*" He grabs the broom and starts sweeping the wood floors, then the black and white-speckled linoleum kitchen floor. "Does he ever help out?" He kneels to whisk two tiny piles.

"Hah!" Melissa says, "maybe if it's cloudy."

115

The microwave beeps, and Casper starts then serves Melissa a bowl of chicken soup.

Then he ties off a Publix bag from under the kitchen sink, fits a new one in the green wastebasket.

"Boy, is he spoiled. Does he have a lot to learn or what?" he calls back from the far end of the house, a different Publix bag in hand filled with trash. Back in the kitchen, he lines the bags up on the floor. "Say, you'd like a little more tea, hon? Peppermint? Chamomile? No caffeine, right? Lemme just wash my hands first." He displays his hands as if to a first grade teacher and notices the line where his sleeves end.

He's never noticed before.

He plucks a Land's End catalog dripping with oatmeal out of the garbage, holds it next to his wan forearm and compares it with the bronze one of the model on the cover.

"What kind, hon? Your favorite? Lapsang souchong? Little honey? Milk? Steamed?"

"Sure dear, that'd be fine," Melissa says. "I'm *so* lucky I'm married to you. I really ask too much, but you never complain. Can you imagine poor Luz?" she switches to a Tagalog accent, Yul Bryner as the King of Siam, Bloody Mary on Bali Hai, *"You like chill beer, honey, you favorite. Dos Equis. I prop you feet up, rub dem, change channel?"*

"Don't they have a goddamned remote?" Caper says.

"Sure, of course, but it tires his finger and spoils the manicure. *Yeah, that'd be great, my manicure, hon, can you put it on 132, the game."* Melissa pats her hand on the table, mimicking him. *"Here, come watch it with me. Good, but as long as you're quiet…,"* Then Melissa pantomimes Anna dipping her head below Yul Bryner's.

"Wow," Casper uncoils the vacuum cord, "sorry dear, I'm gonna make a little noise for a sec, hope it doesn't bother you. I know you're sensitive." His big gut gets in the way when he bends for the "on" button, and he is

117

perturbed.

discomfited

That he must smash it down

Suck it in.

"OK, no problem," she says, "Don't be too long. Say, I mean after you finish, of course, when you have time, later, not now, I mean, can you draw me a bath? I'm pretty tired, and…," and there, in her eyes again, that odd six-segment Drosophila texture, a faraway look, the wanton look of a fruit fly dive bombing an overripe banana.

"Sure," Casper says, "soon as I get done with this." And he wrangles the vacuum cord, "Y'know when you think about it, *he* must be more miserable than her. I mean where's the satisfaction, the meaning in his life? Must be bored outta his mind, useless, guilty, deep down inside, don't ya think?" But Caper's voice is plaintive, supplicating. He's a first-grader again, fingernails splayed out to teacher, teacher poised with metal-edged ruler

High

High

Higher

Ready

To

Bring

Down

"Don't ya think he must feel an enormous guilt, like some pimp, dealer, cipher, eunuch…?"

Even higher

Higher

The ruler goes

And

"…desperate, don't ya think? A certain desperation?" Casper flinches.

"Um…well…," she says.

"How can he possibly not? Well, then, he's in for a rude realization, sooner than later. It's all gonna come crashing down on him like a house of cards," Casper looks up at her imaginary ruler, "as sure as his six pack must someday deflate."

"Ya think?" she says, "I dunno; some people are just wired that way."

He flicks on the vacuum.

Then he boils the water, spoons out a dollop of honey, rummages for the lapsang souchong, scoops it into the tea ball—she only likes it loose.

"Just built that way, y'think?" he says.

"Can you really fill it up, honey? I like it strong, strong and dark, y'know, can you really pack it in there, give it an extra dollop. Like it strong... dark."

"Sure, honey, extra tea

Extra dollop

Iota

Smidgen

Moiety

Ration

Jot

Tittle

Scintilla

Snippet

Strong

And

Dark

Strong

And

Dark

Casper lets fly the chrome tea ball, the lapsang souchong tea, *and* the extra dollop.

Strong

And

Dark

Lets it fly like a line drive to short, out straight over the kitchen island, horizontal across the red geometric Bokhara, leaving a wake of black leaves like the swath of an F-5 Tornado, then a bounce off the white sheet rock like a homer robbed by the 318 foot left field wall.

"You okay?" Melissa says.

"Sorry, hon, yeah, yeah, I'm fine, okay, it just sorta slipped outta my hand," he kneels on the red Bokhara with a pink whisk broom and pan. "I'll clean it up, I'll get it, I just thought for a sec, well, I was just imagining, just wondering, gee, my skin *is* kinda...

Melissa glances at the model on the cover of a Land's End catalogue. Her lips form an imminent, inchoate "s" sound.

"Sallow," he says, "y'know, maybe I *should* work on my tan a little and...,"

"Work on your what?"

"My tan, y'know," he studies his pasty forearm.

"You look fine; besides, remember what the dermatologist said, and...,"

"Yeah, the dermatologist...I know...but...," Casper rubs his porcelain forearms, looks from

122

them to the Land's End cover. Several times. Then he considers his toes. His poor toes, ensconced, imprisoned, Chinese bound feet, in those tan Desert Boots. He bends, rubs the burning toes beneath the suede, rubs, closes his eyes, imagines. "Ahhhhhhh," he sighs.

"Say, honey," Melissa opens her eyes wide,

"honey,

you're…

not…

jealous…

are…

you?"

"Jealous?" he looks up from his toes.

"Jealous. You're not jealous of *Stanley*, are you?"

"Stanley? Is that his name? Stanley? Me?" He can't decide *what* to rub…his pale forearm? His constricted toes? His bloated gut? "Me? Ridiculous! This *Stanley's* in for a rude awakening, a very rude awakening. She'll come around. Soon enough…she'll…,"

"Uh, honey, that bath? I mean, of course, when you have time, when you have a chance, you were gonna…,"

Casper ties off the Publix bag with the Land's End catalog now inside, the model's rectus abdominus clinging to the wet plastic and peeking through. He tugs the knot tighter and tosses the whole thing into the trash.

Then, he kneels by the bath.

"Not too hot, right hon?" he calls out, one hand on a squeaky handle, the other gauging the stream of water.

MISS GLYCOLOSIS

"Yo, Mr. Thing, when are we ever going to use this stuff?" Courtney Smith, a student.

T ap...Tap...Tapping. Georgette texting.
Teen Vogue on lap. Earphone in right ear.
Eyeballs doing triple gainers.

"Got coded today," she shoves the Huge Bio Text across the table with fingertips as if it's a dirty toilet sponge.

"Let's take a look," I say. "Coded?"

She stands, snaps arms to her sides, thumbs protruding a hand below denim cutoffs.

"Well…?"

"Mr. Reid's just pickin' on me. I can't help it if my arms are long."

I pull the Huge Bio Text toward me; it's odd, with anticipation; a lover returning into my trembling arms after a long absence. *How you've changed! How not!*

"Well…what page?"

The inky bouquet?

The chalky hue?

The fine font?
The heft of a nested stack of 4 wax-lined dissection pans?

The swish of its silken pages on flesh?

The intricate diagram, a Hindu bride's mehndi?

Why do I shiver like the groom peeking, forbidden, through a jeweled curtain?

I want to stroke this thangka

This double-folded

Ten-armed

Ten-legged Kali

Miss September

Miss Glycolosis.

It's a plain, meticulous, lab-goggle spidery font, yet on *my* retinas intertwining vines, gold leaf filigree.

It's ten ox-herding pictures, ancient runes, hieroglyphics, carved, copulating couples on a Hindu temple, a sinuous staff of the music of the spheres, a Milky Way swath through the night sky.

I probe it, the tiny scarlet phosphoruses, P's, a blind man caressing lover's face, nipples, areolae, soft fine hairs, fondling this Vibuti, this gold dust between thumb and forefinger.

"Glycolosis," I say it aloud.

127

Isolde

Juliet

Layla

Heloise

Eurydice

Lakshmi

"Glycolosis," I say again.

"Gly...what?" Georgette snatches the tome away, slams it shut, bends over her iTouch, Art Tatum attacking the ivories.

"No!" I snatch it back, pry it open with both hands. "Look, all you gotta remember is...two ATP's in, *four* out." My finger eddies around a red "P" then taps.

Tap

Tap

Tap

Tap

"Two in, *four* out."

Tap

Tap

Tap

Tap

"Uh, look dad, I gotta buy some clothes; can we go to Target? The mall?"

"Clothes? You've got plenty of clothes," I stab a red "P."

Tap

Tap

Tap

Tap

"Just try to remember…two ATP's in, *four* out.

It's quite a miracle.

You'll do fine."

"Two ABC's in, *four* out. Okay, I got it. Is that all? Now can we…?"

"A…T…P's," I say.

"Whatever." Her fingers on her iTouch are Keith Jarrett on a Steinway.

Tap

Tap

Tap

Tap

Miss Glycolosis. Like she's never left…so long ago. I've studied her, taught her--true, in her *simplified* form—re-created her, term after term, in colored chalk, yellow hydrogens, red phosphoruses, blue ATP's. She could have hung, held her own, brass-plaqued, twixt Dubuffet and Picasso. But each term I lost her, a purple-y brown sponge water, as ephemeral as Franklin's fly, swirling down the slop sink drain. So nice to see her again; I shan't let her go, no, not this time.

And her

Py-

Ru-

Vates…

"Pyruvate," I flip to the next page, pastel baby blue.

My index finger and the pyruvate the two digits in Michelangelo's "Creation of Adam."

> "Pyruvate! It becomes…,"
> But she hops back as if from a cottonmouth in the tall grass.

> "Py…what?" Georgette's scooping her iTouch, Teen Vogue, makeup into a blue paisley Vera Bradley bag as if an earthquake siren has sounded.

> "…becomes…well, never mind…it's the Krebs Cycle."

> "Dad, I really haven't got a thing," says the back of her yellow Abercrombie T-shirt.

I go for the Hail Mary, flipping to page three, the last diagram, the color of lemon junket.

"Then, *this* gets used *here*." My finger traces an arc in the air. "Nothing's wasted, you see? It's a model of efficiency. One might almost think…well…," and I'm channeling Carl Sagan. "My God, thirty-four ATP'S!" As I touch them, all thirty-four in turn, each one, like some stations of the cross, I feel their electricity tingle, course up through my fingertips; my heart races; my face flushes. "Oxidative phos…Do you realize?"

"Uh, later, dad. Mall tomorrow?"

Her earphones are in, her blue Vera Bradley is slung over her yellow shoulder; her iTouch is in her right hand, her left hand going like McCoy Tyner on a Bosendorfer.

"It's

Called

Oxidative

Phos…,

Oh, hell!" I massage the pudding-yellow page, smooth it out, then fold the text shut. With both palms, I scoop it up like a *Holy Granth* bound for its night's chamber on a silver palaver. Lay it down on the laminated wood kitchen table, like a *Holy Granth* on a red silk pillow.

Like a *Rig Veda* on a blue silk teakwood altar.

Georgette slings her quiz at me a few days later.

"Hey dad, I did pretty well, hunh?"

"Oh?"

"Yeah, Mrs. Cocorikas makes it real interesting, real…uh…relevant."

"Oh?" I say.

"Yeah, real simple."

REAL LIBERATION THEOLOGY

"Language—the spoken word—has a vibration. Written words also have a vibration. Anything in existence has a vibration." Masaru Emoto

Neneng, a Buddhist monk from Manila, innocent face, eyes as blue as a baby doe's, a starched wimple and habit to match, so vulnerable, reads aloud from the purple grammar book on her desk.

"The teach… *blank*"—she actually says "blank"—"the teacher *blank* that to the student."

The class—dentists, lawyers, doctors, nurses, perhaps a minister or two from around the planet —titters. And on a wall map, a grid of red stick-pins as thick and regular as the little wooden balls in a cabbie's ventilated seat cushion wafts in an ill wind, that same wind that sets dogs to braying hours before the tsunami hits.

"Okay, okay, Neneng, now try it again, but please use the modal *should* plus the verb *to say,*" suggests her teacher, Dr. Elieezer.

"Uh, the teacher shouldn't have *says* that to the student," Neneng tries, her cheeks whistling as if punctured with leaking air holes.

Elieezer smiles, but his blue and red silk rep tie lays a tad *off* on his button-down blue oxford, blue blazer's brass buttons not quite as shiny, half-specs ride crooked on his nose, ironed chinos not quite as crisp as usual. He fellates a cheap Bic pen, and his

William F. Buckley snake tongue slither is a tad arrhythmic, like a bad heartbeat.

His heart palpates like the needle readout from a tsunami buoy in the South China Sea.   He lists like a breached tuna boat.

The nightmare!

Again!

"Uh, well, not exactly. Would you like to try again?"

Neneng casts blue eyes downward, clears her throat, and Elieezer checks his watch behind his own purple text, yellow sticky notes sprouting from all sides like Raggedy Ann hair tufts.

"The teacher shouldn't have *saying* that?" Neneng asks.

"Uh, Neneng, well, don't forget, it's modal plus *base*, should eat, should sleep, should see…right?"

Elieezer feels it coming, that night mare…

So verboten

Yet

Somehow

So

Exhilarating.

"Right," says Neneng, "In Manila, uh, we don't, uh...the teacher shouldn't *said* that to the...,"

"Neneng,

the modal

Plus

The...,"

It's Teilhard de Chardin's omega tipping point, photon reaching threshold energy, proton kicking off nuclear cascade, prodromal inguinal *compromise* giving way in a hot tear, patellar tendon snapping, Achilles' tendon ripping, aneurysm popping, acid kicking in, bottom falling out.

Something gives way in poor Elieezer.

Thirty-odd years of holding back.

Why *wouldn't* the floodgates open?

And *so few years left* to do it.

Always there.

Nothing to find.

Awake.

Buddha nature.

But what matter why?

He's finally

Letting

His

Freak

Flag

Fly!

"Uh, Neneng,

    it's the modal

    plus

the…,

He says *it*.

Base form.

The…

His top teeth over his lower lip, he says *it*
again.

Base form.

Neneng blanches

Her once dark face a puffy white cloud
framed by her sky-blue wimple.

Thirty students

Wait

Shift

Rustle pages

All eyes on Dr. Elieezer.

They've heard it before, these *aliens*. L'il Wayne, strange, alien, too, more extra-planetary than Sun Ra and his Space Arkestra, is no stranger to the iPods of their melting pot children.

Neneng flips open her cell phone…,

Dr. Elieezer's a goner, a condemned man on the gurney, wrists together held out in front of himself, eyes clamped tight.

Waiting

Waiting

For *them*.

Just like in the bad dream

Dr. Manny plucks the medals from his chest, the sword from his scabbard; they'll clink at his feet, kick up little puffs of dry dirt. Then, *they'll* take him away.

…but then she flips it closed.

For Elieezer's strangely peaceful,

confess-ed

purged

unburdened

a smile playing on his top-teeth-over-bottom-lip.

And, when he parts his eyes, his students, first Neneng, calm returning to her child-like face, tentatively, hand demurely shielding her lips; then another, then all, Colombian lawyers, and Korean doctors, and Russian dentists, and Chinese judges, and Egyptian soccer players, and Iranian business women, smiling, all of their top teeth over their bottom lips.

"Gee," Elieezer says, "Gee, this is…,"

And he says *it* again

"great. This is…,"

He even exaggerates, modeling the top teeth over lower lip

F-f-f-first

F-f-f-finger

F-f-f-free

It's an Oprah teachable moment as all eyes are on his lips. The chanting builds to a crescendo, a glorious Tower of Babel.

The classroom walls vibrating.

The word bent, twisted, manipulated, a Peanuts cartoon on Silly Putty, stretched, compressed, like the universe itself, forward, backward

Deconstructed

Impotent

Powerless

Metal bent to fatigue

Donor fatigue

Defrocked priest

Defanged cobra

Ca…

Thar…

Sis!

Elieezer's relief is as contagious as H1N1.

"We learn good curse word, yes?" Neneng whistles. "Teach us another."

"Yeah," Elieezer grins, and he's contorting his wet lips into a librarian's *shhhhhhhhhh*, when suddenly the class droops like a tomato vine in a hard freeze.

Dr. Manny, standing, not a little hunched over, next to the red security phone by the doorway, is stabbing at the vents in the asbestos ceiling.

"Uh, Dr. Elieezer," he speaks as if analyzing a funding grant. "Can you keep it down a bit?" But in the instant it takes him to turn towards the red phone, he scans the faces of Dr. Elieezer's students, ending at Neneng, who grins at him through lips still frozen in the librarian *shhhhh*.

Manny's hand catches in midair, micro millimeters from the red phone, then swoops up to his green silk rep tie, which he unbuttons, and he springs up erect as if Atlas suddenly unburdened of his globe.

"Hey, not bad Dr. Elieezer," he salaams the class. "Okay, here's another one for you guys," he elbows Elieezer playfully, and his lips curl into a "*shhhhh.*"

Thirty-one pairs of librarian lips, strained from grinning ear-to-ear, do their best to mimic him.

And the filigree of sound

Shhhhhhhhhhh

Wafts

Harmlessly

Up

Into

The

Ventilation duct

An arabesque of

Steam

Hissing

Cleanly

Antiseptically

From an

Autoclave.

THE CHINESE LESSON

"When we open the hand of thought, the things made up inside our heads fall away…all our troubles disappear." Kosho Uchiyama

*L*ao shi…teacher. *Jiao shou*…professor. Professor Wei Ping in Wal-Mart black slacks and a red short-sleeved V-neck cotton sweater climbs atop a red leather desk chair shoved up close to the window. On her, these dowdy clothes positively radiate. From that window on the twenty-third floor in her Waldorf Hotel room, standing tiptoe, leaning precariously close, craning her neck, she catches a glimpse of Marco's building with the wooden water tower; she tingles. It swoops hyperbolically up from Forty-Second Street like the Three Gorges Dam, across from the pair of stone lions guarding the library. *His* water tower, that holds the water, that goes to the fountain, that Marco bends in front of, that wets *his* moist lips.

The chair wobbles, and she nearly tumbles, plummets out the window, twenty-three stories down to Park Avenue.

"Oh my god," she grabs a towel rack, "*Ai ya!*" climbs down, smoothes out her black hair, re-ties her ponytail.

She is at once relieved yet profoundly disappointed.

An hour earlier, on the way to the hotel, she came to think of Marco as even more special if such were possible. She'd confused the Brooklyn-

Queens-Expressway with the Cross-Bronx
Expressway, like juxtaposing her own Inner and
Outer Ring Roads. English was impossible; she
was a helpless baby. Oh, poor Marco. The cabbie,
from Mumbai, one hand outstretched, refused to
pop the trunk, relinquish her bags.

"One-hundred-thirty-seven dollars!"

That's what she *thought* he'd said; perhaps it was
three-hundred-seventeen.

She paid up and finally understood, or so she
thought, that look in Marco's eyes. How hard it
was for him. No wonder she'd wanted to take care
of him. But, oh, the terrible shame.

Most would have turned around right then and
there, hopped the first plane back to Beijing, but
she, Professor Lao Shi Wei Ping, became only more
determined. She twisted off her platinum wedding
band and stowed the pictures from her wallet--
YuTing and her three girls--in a drawer in the desk
in the hotel room.

YuTing, Beijing University physics professor,
dear, sweet husband with a rice bowl—*fan wan*—

haircut. She tingles when she recalls tousling the fan wan; he, mock serious, swatting her away.

Then shudders, for she's told him it's a conference.

A tale to rival Zhang Yimou.

The World Organization for Teachers of Chinese.

Indeed, there is a conference.

But, what she's failed to mention to YuTing,

Slip of the tongue

Slight oversight

So busy; it escaped me; what was I thinking?

Chinese classes

Tai Chi classes

I've simply forgotten

Perfectly normal

Could happen to anyone

Run of the mill

Failed to mention to YuTing, father of my three children, our three children, Hui, Xiao, and Min, all four point oh students in prestigious American universities

The conference

Is two floors

Below

Marco's

Office.

Perfectly reasonable slip-up.

Racing down Vanderbilt, around Grand Central, now, she remembers the first time; her knees go weak in black poly slacks, and she leans against a papier mache'd lamppost.

She was teaching modals, *kuh-ee, dei.* Asked a few students to come to the board. When Marco stood, grasped the chalk, even an idiot could tell he *too* practiced Tai Chi. Those tight jeans. *Lan nu zai ku,* cowboy pants. That dark green painted-on shirt, flap pockets, open two buttons. Two leather and cowrie shell surfer boy necklaces.

Had he worn them just for her?

Short-cropped blond hair.

And the smile, genuine, open, enigmatic, Buddha-like.

And the green eyes, if possible, even more open, genuine, round, sparkling, smoldering, mesmerizing. So exotic, so un-Chinese. Yet, like a Tai Chi master's eyes. How could he not know?

She was on hands and feet, traversing a bottomless crevasse on an aluminum ladder across the dreaded Khumbu Icefall. Yet, strange, she'd never signed up for the expedition.

"Sure Professor Wei Ping. I'll try, *hun hao,*" Marco said in terrible Chinese, so needy, helpless but reached for the chalk so nonchalantly, as if, well, as if he were just reaching for a piece of chalk.

Ai ya, my God, so tall, so un-Chinese-edly tall as he wrote.

And now, turning right on Forty-Second Street, five and a half years, one thousand-three-hundred-seventeen students later, the exact sentence, his dreadful *fan ti zi,* Chinese characters, the chalk dust rivulets just now, still drifting down the blackboard.

Ni de kuh-ee suour Chong wun, he scrawled.

"We can speak Chinese," or perhaps, "The green apples are English" or maybe...?" still echoing off the green classroom walls.

The click of her chalk on the board, tapping each hieroglyphic character

Tap

Tap

Tap

"Excellent

Excellent

Excellent writing, Marco."

And she attempted to deflect suspicion, glowered at the three ditzy blonds from Florida, themselves gaga over Marco, who caught her staring at him.

"I hope you're taking notes?"

Anyway, they would never understand. Couldn't possibly appreciate the *special* bond between herself and Marco. Almost a son, or…?

They *dare* not!

"Shei shei ni, Lao shu Wei Ping." The power of Marco's intense green Tai Chi master eyes —"Thank you teacher Wei Ping"--could match that of the Three Gorges Dam and then some.

Now, passing the twin stone lions on her left, she recalls the *last* time. After class, just before he left Beijing, he'd come with a question about the *le* marker, the present perfect. That's what he'd told her, anyway. He'd edged his chair close. His Old Spice, like a powerful insecticide, obliterated any last vestiges of her English.

"Molly and I wanted you to have this," he said in dreadful Chinese and handed her a blue Sydney Opera House Sno-globe. "Got it on our honeymoon."

Professor Wei Ping shook the globe and pretended her wince was for his bad Chinese.

"Honeymoon?"

"My new wife, Molly," Marco said.

Wife? But can she...? And why does he look at me that way?

"I'll treasure it forever," she shook the globe again.

One last time.

Now, just across Avenue of the Americas, as formidably raging as the Yangtze in flood, her heart aflutter, hand trembling, sweating like a school girl with a crush. Marco's behind the glass door with the green sign, a Starbucks.

Is it the summer furnace heat?

Terminal jet lag?

Rot gut diner coffee in Peacock Alley?

The five bucks a cup?

H1N1 onset?

The burning asphalt tugs at her black canvas slippers; the metal handle sizzles.

Thank god.

She hesitates, and lets it go.

Almost turns around.

155

But no, she takes a deep breath, swaddles her hand in her red silk scarf and yanks.

Whoosh of AC, coffee, orange scones, Miles Davis, hissing espresso. Eyes adjust to mustard walls, black-shirted, green-aproned baristas.

And, Marco's green eyes peeking over the top of a Venti Iced Mocha—*his* drink…*their* drink!—tongue licking foamy whipped creamy lips.

But something's different.

"*Zao shang hao,*" he calls across the brown tile floor, his neck veins popping, taut against his double leather choker.

"You…remember…me?" she calls out, in Chinese.

She steadies herself on one table, then another, as if working her way through a chest-high cypress swamp in hip boots.

"Wait," she smiles, "I'll be right back." She motions with her blue silk wallet at Marco's cup. "Venti Iced Mocha, right?"

"How'd you…?" Marco double takes.

A small reddish cup, a kid's Crème Caramel Brulee, intercepts her turn towards the counter.

"How the hell'd you...?" He speaks English, and something's different in his beautiful green eyes. He's a man in his element.

The owner of the red cup, a boy, a mini-Marco in every detail, down to the double leather thong necklace, winds over from the bathroom.

"Dad?" He sips his Crème Brulee, "Dad?"

"This is Professor—*Lao Shi* Wei Ping," Marco begins, "She...,"

The boy looks at her, his dad, back at her again. The boy's eyes are green Tai Chi master marbles, too.

Lao Shi Wei Ping drops her blue silk wallet.

"Hi...my student...your dad...," Her English, under such intense pressure, implodes upon itself.

And, she's suddenly horrified. She realizes how horribly wrong she's been.

Five and a half years wrong.

So obvious.

Father

Son

It's the same Tai Chi master look that nearly tumbled her into the Khumba Icefall crevasse.

But, in this face-speaking-English, this confident face, it's nothing more, nothing less, father to son.

Can I run all the way to Beijing? She wonders and starts out, east—*dong*--toward the door. But, passing the counter, she slows, then halts.

"*Ting ni...uh...*please...a tea please," her English almost totally routed, making as much sense as a climber deprived of oxygen. "Tea?"

The barista calls over her manager.

Lao Shi Wei Ping glances back at the two Marcos. "No, wait minute. *Dong ee dong. Ni yo mei yo*…you have 'Om'? Same Beijing? 'Om' *cha*…tea? *Wuor she wan*…I like 'Om' tea. *Shei shei.*"

And somehow, a cup of Om tea materializes.

"Meet you nice," she sits with Marco and his son.

"My dad always says what a great *teacher* you are," Marco Junior says and looks at his dad.

Teacher? She's momentarily disappointed. *Only teacher?*

"Learned so much, always speaking Chinese. Drives me and mom nuts," Marco Junior adds.

Lao Shi Wei Ping watches father look at son.

"Yes, he was quite a *student,*" she says. "Very… *special.*"

She stares at little Marco's twin leather and cowrie shell necklaces.

Stares

And stares

And stares

Yet sees just

Twin leather and cowrie shell necklaces.

Her English, though rudimentary at best, is coming back, like a climber descending to base camp.

She understands now.

I knew that! I needn't have worried.

Never any danger.

"Quite the excellent *student,*" her English is flawless now, "when he put his mind to it."

Marco looks at her, quizzically, apologetically, forgivingly, yet without…without…yes…the obsequiousness.

He looks at his son as she might at YuTing, tousling his fan wan haircut. Like YuTing might look at her, swatting her away, mock serious.

A million?

Two?

Ten?

What recompense for a lifer freed through DNA evidence after thirty years?

Just knowing helps.

It's an honest look.

Nothing more.

Nothing less.

Nothing special.

I really did know that!

But, oh, the relief.

Oh, the relief.

SAD NEWS

"There's a place for sadness, which will come in waves. But fundamentally, you'll realize the person, the real part of the person—his essence—does not die. There is no such thing as death." Eckhart Tolle

"Simple really. Sad news…," E. Ann McPherson mops the sweat on her neck, the sweat soaking the collar of her blue denim shirt, sweat making pulp of the double-folded paper towel paper-clipped to her collar, mops the sweat with a neatly folded linen hanky. She kneels in blue jeans in liriope and mulch and plucks weeds.

"Hunh?" Mac Weldon, sweat-soaked, blue-denimed, kneeling and weeding alongside her, screws up his leathery face and mops his white afro with a crumpled red bandana.

"Sad news," Ann reseats her sweat-damp straw hat, "I always wrote 'sad news'…,"

Mac tents his sopping shirt.

"Look, uh, Ellie…it's kinda hot and…," "In my email. Subject line…sad news… guess it wasn't really sad."

Mac tosses a clump of weeds into the bed of a green Cushman stuffed with oily rakes, brooms, shovels, blowers, trimmers.

"They had it in for me…all of 'em…'specially that *Bonnie*…,"

Mac frowns and tosses another clump of weeds.

"Bonnie?" Ellie says, "Assistant dean? Birkenstocks? Cotton yoga pants?"

While she talks, she fixates on a second story office window in the new brick building, a window as dark and opaque as her eyes. Then, with her dirty cuff, she burnishes a little gold pin with a miniscule diamond and the words "20 years" etched across it.

"Anyway…it's not important."

"Uh, Ellie…," Mac inscribes a circle around the liriope bed with his reddish eyes, eyebrows peaked.

"Didn't quite see it my way. Almost got me canned and…,"

"Fired?" Mac asks, and Ellie's cackle wilts the liriope.

Mack shivers in the baking sun, squints against sun and salty sweat.

"What's not sad? Bonnie brought up some half-baked, trumped-up charge…and I was almost history."

Mac swigs from a blue plastic cooler, offers Ellie, who doesn't respond.

"Bonnie told me, 'If you can't think of anything nice to say.' Told me *she'd* just write 'Happy News'.   Happy news? In a friggin' death notice?" Ellie twirls a soil-encrusted fingernail at her temple.

Mac tries to sneak away around a corner of the brand new red brick building, but Ellie grabs his wet sleeve.

"Have it right here…," Ellie crinkles pink tablets, jingles god-knows-what-else in her pockets.

And a slip of paper

A Dead Sea Scroll

A piece of parchment

Papyrus

A page from the Guttenberg Bible

A scrap of paper folded so often, folded to nose blowing suppleness

She accordions it, a dozen sheets, like mosaic tiles, hanging by threads, limp in the still wet air. She smoothes it out between a leaf blower and weed whacker on the truck bed,

A curator her rare document

A proud jeweler her jade

A collector her artifact

But, like flesh way too long on an upholstered Barcalounger, the penciled words have become one with the silken paper, inextricably intertwined, and decipherable only to Ellie.

"See?" she peers over spectacles as scratched as a taxi partition, then holds it out to Mac.

"Bonnie's email. Blah, blah, blah, blah…," she punctuates each "blah" with a flick.

"'There-flick

Is-flick

No-flick

Death-flick'."

Pause

"No death?!"

Mac's about to yank his arm away when Tito, their boss, crawls by in a green golf cart, left to right, and waves. Mack, relieved, scurries for his rake.

"Ain't nuthin' funny 'bout it," Mac says. "Can't argue with you there, Ellie."

Hunched over her own rake, Ellie looks good. The out-of-doors, the physical labor suit her. Her face glows. She looks comfortable in her skin. Her sweat is pure, flushed, clean. Sauna sweat. Steam room perspiration. The sweat of a cave wall, of an icy glass of lemonade, of a Lakota i-ni-pi purification ceremony, a Mexican tem-az-cal, a sweat lodge. Outdoor sweat, ballet sweat, a lover's sweat.

Her salubriousness is not an ironman's frantic, forced, febrile fitness. Her sweat not football sweat, stinky flop sweat, the self-conscious stew-in-your-own-juices sweat of a thesis defender, of a job interviewee. Nay, not indoor sweat nor onanist's sweat.

"Two weeks paid leave they gave me," Ellie goes on. "'Bout drove me nuts. No fourteen-hour days, no phones, no weekend retreats, no meetings, no bottomless 'in' box, nuthin', no distraction, horrible! I was a junkie jonesing for a fix. I couldn't quiet *it*. Couldn't turn *it* off. Couldn't silence *it*. 'Bout went off the deep end!"

She massages the silky paper between fingertips like a puffy-cheeked squirrel hunched over its acorn, fingertips at lips, *it's mine, it's mine, it's mine*...and lets out another liriope-wilting cackle.

When Tito crawls by again, right to left, and glowers, she stuffs the grimy paper in her sweaty armpit, and she and Mac wield their rakes like Olympic curlers.

"Too much damned time to think about *it*. And, I also realized I hated my job. Hated it, but couldn't do without it!"

Mac leans on his rake and rolls his eyeballs.

"I woulda given it all up in a second, but I couldn't. I envied *her, she* could; *she* knew how to relax. But, I didn't. I was trapped. I needed that damned job. But, I dreaded going back."

Mac grabs a huge plastic shovel and "tsk, tsk, tsk's."

Ellie rakes; Mac scoops.

Then they rifle through the truck bed for two push brooms, which they pilot two-handed, with small, easy, paid-by-the-hour strokes, meditative strokes.

Zen strokes

Restorative

Peaceful

Bristle scrape on concrete

Phit

Phit

Phit

They sweep up the walkway

They chop wood, carry water.

"Two weeks after I get back," Ellie leans on her broom, "Bonnie lost her mom. Cancer, terrible, long, drawn-out, hospice, awful death."

Ellie's knuckles whiten on her broom handle at the thought of *it* as if clutching an ice axe in an avalanche.

"Let *me* go in my sleep."

"Unh, hunh," Mac nods.

"Bonnie wrote the obit herself and put the words *'sad news'* in the subject line. She came by my office blubbering like a baby. 'It *is* so sad. I miss her so much. You were *so* right!'"

But, *I* suddenly understood and scratched over her subject line with a Sharpie. "Happy News," I read it to Bonnie. "Can't you see? It's happy news."

Now Ellie's knuckles around the broom handle regain their color; her eyes lighten; there's a bit of green in them after all.

Mac's leaning on the cornerstone of the building, and when he checks his watch, he notices the carved inscription. With each name he reads aloud, he blots at his sweaty neck with his bandana:

Governor

Mayor

Congressman

President

Of

The

College

Eleanor

Ann

McPherson

"Ellie?" he says.

Eleanor Ann McPherson pretends to be rummaging through the truck bed for a blower.

"Ellie?" he asks again.

She tilts back her damp straw hat, mops her forehead with the linen hanky.

"And Bonnie?" Mac asks.

Mac's reddish eyes follow her green eyes to that dark and opaque office window in the new building.

In profile, Ellie strikes a Lincoln-on-a-penny pose,

A

Decidedly

Presidential

Pose.

THE PHONUS BALONUS

"We will also discover how to be friendly with the ego and dissolve it." Dr. David Hawkins

A-ya-fat-la-yo-kut-l, too, began small. One day, nuthin', the tiny glass knob of a stainless steel percolator of Maxwell House on a low burner, blurp, blurp, blurp. Next day, what the hell? Old man Stefansson's farm swallowed up by hot lava.

"God's will," Hjalmarsson rests on his staff and puffs his pipe.

"Bull crap," Stefansson mutters.

One Tuesday, "A Course in Miracles" is spread open, blue, on Peter Petard's lap. He's swathed in dark, quiet, Fortress of Solitude, cone of silence, monotonous but secure drone of Indian harmonium. All perfect, numinous, Peter's part of the whole, I am that, Tat tvam asi, we're all one. He *loves* the driver--a bald Spanish guy with one earring and a very smooth touch on the pedal— loves him as his fellow man.

And he *thinks* he loves those distraught A-ya-fat-la-yo-kut-l-ians and these frantic grounded fliers on the *Times* beneath his blue book.

But when he goes back to his blue book, underlines a passage, and his green marker bleeds

174

through the onion skin page, it breaks the spell…a pebble in his shoe…a bad taste in his mouth.

A-ya-fat-la-yo-kut-i-ans?

Stranded fliers?

The Spanish driver lurches to a stop, and Peter's face slams into the blue plastic seat; his green pen arcs up and then is lost forever between the rancid grooves in the rubber floor. Still, he reaches down, bethinks himself, and when he straightens, is face-to-face, eye-to-eye, mano-y-mano with Chuck.

But, at first, he doesn't recognize him or doesn't *want* to recognize him.

Chuck's ratty beard, scraggly hair, tattered Magic cap…all gone and it's a going-for-an-interview-Sunday-best Chuck who pumps Peter's hand like a crack pipe,

175

"Peter, Buddy, great to see you."

"Same here," Peter lies.

And the driver's swivels and his earring wiggles and glints red.

Peter cinches his blue sweatshirt hood while Chuck drunk-a-logs in Palatka patois. Peter wishes he were *anywhere* else. Even the proctologist would do tagging his inflamed prostate, stabbing it like a runner digging cleats into the third base bag... OUCH!

Chuck extends arms, crosses bony wrists,

"Nuthin as bad," he concludes, sotto voce, "as when they slap on those cuffs.

Bam!" and bows his head.

"I hear ya," Peter lies, eyes the door and pulls the cord.

He leaps from the bus as if down a flaming evacuation chute onto the tarmac, then bobs and feints, a sixty-yard touchdown run through a phalanx of charging headlights, Pamplona bulls, stampeding buffalo, Chuck snapping at his heels.

Wednesday, A-ya-fat-la-yo-kut-l has gone exponential, doubled at least. Padding to the bathroom, Peter empathizes with the grounded passengers if only because Chuck has *him* hostage, Peter's very own personal turbine-destroying ash cloud. He leafs through a system-wide bus schedule.

Yet, he's jealous too. He flicks the morning paper. *They* get cruise ships to take *them* where *they're* going. And, anyway, shouldn't *they* understand?—*he* understands—"don't *you* get it?" he says, "*I* get it! It's just the will of…"

Just

The

Will

Of...

And he fans the schedule

Will

Of...

And he flicks the paper

Just

The

Will

Of...

Until, that is, until suddenly, the game changes, "What the...?" He drops the schedule—it's of no help anyway. *That* was not there last night.

"You must realize...," he persists for a second longer but then the *Times* too falls to the tiled floor; he tries to ignore *it*, addressing the newspaper instead, "It's simply the will of..."

What the hell *is* this...? His...house...of...cards...wobbles...flutters...then...pancakes. His inner tube aneurysms, his hose springs a leak. Something down *there* has *spilled out.* How else to describe it?

Now *this* is a mini a-ya-fat-la-yo-kut-l of his very own.

He waddles to the bus, the same bus, what choice does he have?--giving himself a dose of his own medicine, stroking his blue book like a genie's bottle, "Everything for a reason..."

179

On the bus, Peter lists forty degrees starboard, the least painful angle, a foundering Titanic, his blue capuchin's hood, his blue book are his ramparts, his "Do Not Disturb" on the motel door.

"Buddy," Chuck smiles.

Peter squirms, rivets eyes into his blue book, flips its onion skin pages frantically, tries to render himself invisible.

"Hey, Buddy, you try witch hazel?"

Peter drops his green pen, kicks it out of sight and spends a good two minutes rummaging around for it.

"Witch hazel, dude," Chuck persists. "Been there, done that."

"You say something?" Peter mumbles from between his knees.

"Said Witch hazel."

"Witch hazel?"

Peter's stop is looming. If he doesn't surface now…,

"Yeah, works wonders," Chuck beats him to the cord.

"No kiddin'? Witch hazel."

"Cotton pad and witch hazel,"

Peter's urge to run vanishes.

"…say," Chuck goes on, "what's that blue book you allus readin'?"

"This?" Peter taps it, "Oh, Uh, nuthin'."

Peter tags close to Chuck,

Bonnie and Clyde

Abbott and Costello

Astaire and Rogers

Butch and Sundance

Gilbert and Sullivan

Laurel and Hardy

Lewis and Clark

Lennon McCartney

Simon and Garfunkel

Tracey Hepburn

Yin

And

Yang

"Yeah, little witch hazel, cotton pad and…"

By Monday, Peter's a-ya-fat-la-yo-kut-l is imploding

Laws of Thermodynamics broken

a reverse time lapse.

A Deflating Bozo the Clown punching bag

Collapsing thumb push puppet

After the party bounce house

post coital flaccid priapus,

blow out

collapsed cake,

dynamited demolition,

stricken heap of 3-ring big top tent

Berlin Wall,

Soaked Wicked Witch of the West

I'm melting, I'm melting…

sand castle

gravitied breasts

snowman

startled turtle

And a white-coated proctologist peruses an MRI, scratches his crew cut.

"Hmmmm." He tilts the MRI. "It's a miracle!" But his voice betrays at once that he feels somehow *upstaged* and that he's concerned about April's Mercedes payment.

It's a miracle indeed.

BABA JI

"Teachers are many, masters few." Osho

Marina bends over a steaming sink, scouring the caked-over spaghetti sauce from a huge black pot, wiping the sweat from her forehead with the back of her forearm. I toss my briefcase onto the leather couch, wait a beat,

"…and then…," I milk the moment.

She scrapes the pot, huffing, scrape, puffing, scrape.

"…and then…," I re-enact Shomar's bow, Shomar's *tika-ed* forehead, his optometrist's orange polyester shirt. I simulate the deep graceful arc but wave off halfway down, waist height, like a fighter pilot peeling off formation.

A drop from Marina's furrowed forehead plops into the sudsy sink.

"Then…," I inscribe the rest of the curve with my arm, "then, can you imagine? Shomar dropped to his knee and touched my feet! 'Baba-ji,' he said, 'Teacher-ji'."

Marina drops the pot, sloshing a tsunami of soapy water across the linoleum counter.

"*That's* a new one." I go on, "We were like Shahrukh and Amitabh in 'Khabie Kushie', y'know? I even did the Amitabh move: tried to stop him, mid-bow, pry him at the shoulder, *oh no you really shouldn't…me? I don't deserve it, please, you needn't. Just an English teacher. Just doing my job.* 'Oh, no, no,' he was having none of it, went all the way.

Swish,

Swish,

Swish,

All

The

Way

Down

To my

Filthy black Asics

Anointing them, priest with a censer. Then
he rose, in a flick of his scarlet eye, and was face to
face with my first, second, and *third* eyes."

Marina drips bubbly water at the sink,
waiting.

"Honey," she interrupts, "Honey…," The
"honey" belies exasperation. "Honey," she nods
her perspiration-beaded chin down towards the
soapy sink, towards its submerged tower of crusty
pots and dishes. "…were you, uh, *baba-ji*, uh, were
you thinking of helping?"

"But…?" I protest.

187

"Sometime today, perhaps, *teacher-ji?*" she says.

"But...?" I'm staring at Shahrukh, his head brushing the hem of Amitabh's gold-trimmed, white dhoti kurta.

Upasangrahan it is called.

Would he, Amitabh, wash crusty pots, risk staining his gold-trimmed, white dhoti kurta? And surely, Shahrukh would not allow it, would nudge him aside, roll up his own sleeves, spare baba-ji.

Or perhaps Priti, my beautiful, purple-sari-ed student with a penchant for overusing the present progressive...,

"Priti, perhaps *teacher-ji* can help you; 'love' is a stative verb. I love you, not I'm loving you."

...perhaps Priti, right over there next to Shomar, would step in. Priti, long black hair flowing like the Ganges, dark eyes, third eyes, as wide as Mother Teresa's welcoming arms. Had Shomar's third eye really been observing, he would have noticed I had been staring the whole time.

Shomar's third eye may have been temporarily occluded, an unpolished jewel, but Marina's third eye—as well as numbers one and two—miss nothing.

"*Teacher-ji, baba-ji,*" she picks up the huge black pot, lets it drip green Palmolive

Drip

Drip

Drip

Then lets it go, clanking, crying like a junked Ford Fiesta dropped from a barge onto a rusty underwater junkyard reef.

"I am needing your help, *teacher-ji,*" she says.

"I

Am

Needing

Your

Help

Right

Now!"

She wipes her chafed hands on her red gingham apron and collapses into a leather chair.

"Oh, and *baba-ji?* Could you fetch me a glass of cold water? Please, *baba-ji?*"

Her modal verb, her *please* grate more than Priti's mangled present continuous. But, baba-ji, teacher-ji, bends over the steaming sink, rolls up blue pin-striped sleeves—no gold and white dhoti kurta sleeves these—then reaches

Deep

Low

Way

Way

Down

Into the steaming sink, the pots and pans groaning like a shifting house, like a freighter splitting at its seams.

STRANGE BEDFELLOWS

"The I of me and the I of you are one and the same I. The I AM that I am is the I AM that you are, because this is the I AM that God is, and God is the I AM which is the I AM of you and the I AM of me."

Joel S. Goldsmith

"Your turn," she says, her finger curling, uncurling like a pink gecko tongue in heat.

Her marshmallow shoes, baby blue smock, all wrong. As wrong as a Bardo Thodol amongst sex toys on a night stand by a red-satined futon in a plywood cubicle at the top of a creaky, Moo Shoo Pork scented staircase.

I kneel to finger the tight weave carpet, concentrating like a blind man counting the knots per square inch in a Bokhara. A superfine weave to ward off body fluids.

Armando, my father-in-law, snores, prana-like, through the nose. Could he think, he'd pronounce the thin blue volume next to the tissues on the blond wood night table...nonsense.

"There is no death?" he would cock his shriveled thumb at his wasted chest. "And what is THIS?"

"But Armando?" I would protest quarter-heartedly.

"Petard? Peter? 5:30?" Constance checks her Timex and bounces on her Jet-Puff shoes, the curve of her thigh flexing, unflexing under her baby

192

blue slacks, her breasts outwitting the discreet blue
smock.

A good-for-nothing call button rests on Armando's
chest, rising, falling, rising, falling with his blue
gown his body collapsed, like a crushed Ford atop
this mechanic's pneumatic lift of a bed. He lays
bamboo flooring eighteen hours at a stretch,
squeezes wasps between his calloused fingertips.

"He'd like that," his daughter, Marina, dabs her
green eyes and holds his hand and nods at a
Holiday Inn sunset above the headboard.

"Up to his knees, staring out to the end of his line,"
I make no effort to subdue my voice. His is a Book
of the Dead, morphine-wafer sleep. Here there are
no food trays clanging, IV's beeping, no carafes of
water. "My god! How long can a man go?" A first
grader knows the answer, but I ponder it like an
eigenvalue equation

In

No

Great

Hurry

to arrive at

Quod Erat Demonstratum.

I raise my hand like a timid schoolboy, look to Armando's inert body as if for permission.

"I'm Peter," I tell Constance, who pivots while commanding, "Come with me."

I follow her down a long hallway flanked by opium den room after comatose room to her functionally austere office smelling of Fabuloso with the aluminum and black vinyl contraption dead-center. She replaces John Tesh with "Bubbling Brook", dials down the light, and her first touch, guiding me in, more the shove of a cop ducking my head into his cruiser, triggers the avalanche.

"Where would you like it?" she purrs, red stilettos, slinky dress, clink of bracelets, hot pink nails.

I'm speechless. Can she sense it?

"OK, OK. I'll just let your body talk to me."

I feign escape and hit my head against a crossbar.

She slams me back down, my Adam's apple crushed by a black vinyl pad.

Her perfume washes over me, and the tiny homunculi on my shoulders argue pro, con.

Her strong fingers on my knotted shoulders send a tingle down to my Muladhara chakra, yet they're the hands of a Zen master, bamboo stick, Chinese calligraphy brush, kindly kindergarten teacher pats, which somehow inflame even more, and the deliberating homunculi reach a fever pitch like wind up cymbal-crashing monkeys.

195

When suddenly the lights and John Tesh both come up, and her hands, like icy metal spatulas now, are prying me out like an overdone pancake.

"Done!" she slaps my shoulder.

But I'm *not* done, I think, and feign sleep.

But, she sprays the machine with Fabuloso, sighs deeply, and her back to me now, crumples the paper towel rudely—as if pocketing a few wadded up twenties--and dunks it into the trash in no uncertain terms.

When I return, Marina's still clutching her father's hand.

"We bought you a Times," she says, crying.

"You like the Times," I say.

His rhythmic siddhi breath alters, skips a beat, almost imperceptibly, an acknowledgment perhaps, or maybe a wink, a chuckle, as if to say, "Yeah, I would've enjoyed that too. Yeah."

Constance waits in the doorway, appointment book in hand, eyeing Marina. It's her turn.

Then his breath shifts again, this time fading, nearly inaudible.

"Would you like me to call…?" a Haitian nurse asks.

"Minister…?" Marina says, "Oh, no. I don't think so. He really doesn't…"

Then his breath ceases, and his face relaxes, at peace, almost smiling.

HONG MAI

"To understand everything is to forgive everything." The Buddha

"Prune," Mr. Larry taps his red dry-erase marker on the word. "In my crossword this morning. Anyone know the word?"

"Prune," says Dat, a Vietnamese monk in a long brown robe, "a dried plum."

"Yeah, great!" Mr. Larry tucks in his chin. "Okay, yeah, but do you know it's also a verb, to trim, to cut away?"

"You mean like cut away dead branch; it make the tree grow…more fruit?"

"Make*s*," Mr. Larry corrects, "Perhaps we should review, final 's', three ways?" Larry scribbles his red dry erase marker. "Now, if the ending's voiceless, it's…

seat-*ssss*,

map-*ssss*,

lake-*ssss*,

sssssss…like air out of a punctured bicycle tube.

Mr. Larry mimes a large donut shape. Dat nods bald head, pretends to understand, but inside, his inner dialogue, it's business as usual:

Seat,

Map,

Lake,

Ignoring the final "s."

I'll never get this.

Larry scribbles again. "If it's voiced, it's...

Seed-ʐʐ,

Star-ʐʐ,

Hole-ʐʐ,

Law-ʐʐ,

Larry rests fingers on Adam's apple as if checking for a pulse, fingers leathery, back of hand cratered with basal cell splotches. He peers over his trifocals, down his long nose, *way* down at Dat, then scratches his own bald head between two purple-y blotches. "No vibration in neck," he says, "then make the bee buzzing sound."

But again, Dat's summiting Chomolungma in a whiteout.

Seed

Star

Hole

Law,

This make no sense,

I'll never

Never be able to teach English.

Dat glances over at Tranh.

Teaching Tranh, tiny Tranh, from Ho Chi Minh City, poor Tranh, so fragile, so vulnerable, so pretty, her small plum-shaped breasts, such a short black skirt! The Buddha would be proud of me.

Her dark eyes meet his, so briefly, so fleetingly, then she turns away. Dat smoothes out the crisp placket of the well-tailored grey kurta he wears beneath his brown robes, and for a brief second, smiles at what he sees in some invisible full-length mirror.

But consternation quickly trumps giddiness as the ample sleeves of his brown robe flap ridicule, dismissal.

"Now," Mr. Larry scribbles, and Dat turns away, "now these, I'm afraid, well memorize." Larry scrunches up eyes as if sighting the crosshairs of some delicate armament.

Dat squirms.

"These use the sound *iz*

Dish-*iz*

Match-*iz*

Class-*iz*

Size-*iz*

Page-*iz*

Judge-*iz*

Now, Larry highlights each with the felted puff of his dry erase,

Sh,

Ch,

S,

Z,

Ge,

Dge.

Dat turns back to face Mr. Larry and pleads silently.

Up at three a.m....father spent six month on that boat, seven year in France...if I fail this test...it my third time...they'll throw me out...taking up someone else seat... just not fair.

It is, too, a massive run-on sentence slithering through Dat's tortured brain.

I must go see Mr. Larry...before the test...talk it over, he'll help me...he my only friend really...the monastery so far, so out in the boonie—Mr. Larry taught me 'boonie'—I never get a chance to practice my English...he'll help me...I know he will... he ha' to...what other chance do I have…he my frien'—the other call me 'monk' and lower voice, turn away as if I'm the headmaster—my mentor, my Sherpa, my lifeline, my only chance…I must see him right after class…today.

The run-on morphs into a comma splice, so *s*-ending-less, so enormous, so egregious that could Mr. Larry see it, he'd outstretch arm, finger towards door, Buddha finger pointing at moon.

"Go! Get out!" he'd say, "We're wasting each other's time."

Dat devolves into a Wattsian quivering, quaking mess of jelly; he's pure run-on, the rules of grammar having escaped as if a flock of frightened doves.

Maybe Tranh—he glances over at tiny Tranh and adjusts the grey collar of his kurta in that chimerical looking glass—maybe Tranh can make things better. She'll fix everything. And Tranh smiles, and he smiles, and they both turn away from each other and from the eyes of the Buddha.

Flop!

Mr. Larry flops a khaki green duffel bag—an American flag patch, the size of a small envelope stitched to one side—on to the long table in front of him.

"Okay guys," he announces.

Dat has gotten to calling his fellow monastics "guys", too.

Slowly,

Purposefully,

Mindfully,

Like a monk,

Like the tensho,

Not one grain of rice misplaced,

Unaccounted for,

The way he teaches them modals,

Like his old algebra teacher in Saigon,

Like a captain ticking off a pre-landing checklist,

Like a monk doing walking meditation,

Larry starts to unzip the bag from its far end.

"Show and tell, guys," Mr. Larry explains, "next assignment, lemme show you how it's done."

With well-rehearsed hands, Mr. Larry pulls out a rubbery mask—two glass-covered fly-eyes, long, ribbed, rubbery elephant-trunk tube, dangling, the whole affair floppy, saggy, like Merrick's hide-bound face. Facing his class, he lays the mask,

Reverentially,

Host on the linen communion table, to the far right, then—moving left—fills the entire table, focused, as he is when he gazes up at the asbestos ceiling if he doesn't know something.

"'Y' a vowel or a consonant?" Is he counting the reflective fins in the fluorescent recesses above? "I'll get back to you."

He's an acolyte tending these orange, white, and red Eucharistic utensils:

Dark grey flight suit, draped Dali watch, soul-less cadaver

White helmet, red chevron, flip-down grey visor, fly-eyes

Faded day-glo orange vest, green canvas straps, "pull here" red knob

Pair of high-lace anti-jungle-rot canvas boots

Brown canvas parachute back pack

Looking up at us, un grand patissier

Le feuille au chocolat sur le Marquise

La piece de resistance

Monsieur Larr-ee, ever-so-gently, like setting a Huey dust-off down in a hot LZ

An old black and white framed photo

Could it be Mr. Larry? The hair, so brown, so full, so short, just a hint of his leaning tower of Pisa stoop, such clear eyes, as yet untarnished by forty-two years of insomnia.

Decked out in everything but the helmet, which is in his left hand; his proud right hand—the hand of any man on the polished hood of his prized white Mercedes—rests on the wing of his *very own* A-4, the Skyhawk, its glass canopy popped open, scooping forward, against the grain.

Mr. Larry's pose dares us, "Go ahead! Say something," about the ridiculous parachute hanging from his ass like a heavy diaper.

O Amitabha! Can it be?

The roundrel on the tail...

It was red, white, and blue in real life.

No, of course not, Amitabha.

Impossible

All the plane have them

Don't be silly

In Mr. Larry's picture, the four red missiles slung under the wings are grey—*Uncle Sang told me they were red*--each the size of Mr. Larry, drooping the wings, vengeful, teeth-baring shark faces painted on their noses, black words scribbled feverishly, severe, indecipherable.

But the shark?

Uncle Sang told me they were so close that morning, early, cooking fire filling the jungle air, tea bubbling, rice steaming, oxen and chicken stirring, so close he could see them, teeth bared. But, no, all the plane have rocket bared shark teeth. You're being silly. It can't be.

Dat's thoughts have deteriorated, no longer even run-ons, now mere fragments, and no final "s" to be found; it's all he can muster.

I ran that morning.

209

Sound of twenty typhoon,

Chicken squawking,

Oxen bellowing,

Yelling,

Screaming,

Crying,

Ran until I was knocked to the ground by a hot,
burning firestorm blast,

When I came to,

When I returned,

There was nothing,

Only a few smoldering scorched tree

Bamboo

Pine

One, maybe two, Hong Mai

Pink Plum!

Uncle Sang couldn't see the pilot face, only the dark grey fly-eye, visor, now flickering bright red and orange, the rubber mask, the red chevron on white helmet forehead.

What are the odd?

Dat leans back; the chair is hard. He sighs, at once relief and acknowledgment of the small sigma of these odds. He looks over at tiny, vulnerable Tranh, wants to wrap her in the billowy, brown sleeves of his robe, then averts his eyes again.

"You guys find something," says Mr. Larry, "that represents your country: a Spanish guitar, ring, beaded necklace, flowery dress, colored dish, glass, wooden flute, woven mat, ceramic monkey, tiger, elephant, Chinese wok, Japanese tea set. Prepare a two-minute speech, just two minutes…,"

Dat shivers at how many *s's* might be contained in two minutes of English, more *s's*, he thinks, than the yellow plum blossoms in Hoang Mai, and he slinks down lower.

"But Mr. Larry?" he says, "it too hard."

211

"Practice it," Mr. Larry ignores him, "front of a mirror, ten, fifteen times, really polish it."

"But Mr. Larry?" Dat pleads.

"You'll stand up here," Mr. Larry taps the black aluminum lectern, "and tell us all about it." Mr. Larry mimes himself at the bathroom mirror, wiping steam with an invisible towel, wrapping it around his middle, laughing at his joke.

The black lectern looks ever-so-flimsy to Dat, and he bends forward to retrieve his huge coned straw hat—the only thing under the seat in front of him. It has a mauve band around it, his sole souvenir of a decade in Plum Village monastery. He's getting the hell out of there.

"Or maybe a black lacquer begging bowl, a saffron robe...

...a

...straw

...hat?"

Mr. Larry intercepts Dat, who plops back in his seat, his brown robe fluttering about him. Part of Dat wants to flee, but he is also trying, with all his strength, to look through a dark grey visor, some Buddha x-ray vision perhaps.

He *must* know.

After class, Dat stalls, rolling up the overhead cord and wheeling the machine into the closet. It's a walking meditation. But when Mr. Larry reaches for the helmet, he abandons the machine and turns to the front.

"Mr. Larry," he squeals, fingering the red chevrons on the white helmet.

"Hundred and first Airborne," Larry strokes the chevrons.

And Dat understands.

"Uh, Mr. Larry. I'd like to bring Hong Mai blossom for show and tell. Is that...?"

Mr. Larry looks up at the neon lights.

"Hong Mai. Pink plum tree. Beautiful. Very rare in my village. Symbol of hope."

"Hong Mai," Larry's lips silently count the reflective vanes in the ceiling lights, "Pink plum. Your village…?" he asks.

And Larry understands, too.

"Haven't been able to sleep for a long time…," Mr. Larry commences. As he talks—over several hours—he seems to straighten up. Dat listens quietly. When Mr. Larry leans back in his chair, all done, Dat asks,

"Now the *s's*. Mr. Larry, can you help me with the final *s* sound? We're having test in two day…," he corrects himself, "two day-ꙅꙅꙅꙅꙅꙅꙅꙅꙅꙅꙅꙅꙅꙅꙅꙅꙅꙅꙅꙅ" and smiles. "I think I need your help."

"Okay Dat," Larry launches into it without pause. "Now, if it's a voiceless ending, the sound is 'sssssssssssssss' like walk-*ssss*, the sound of a snake hi*ssssssssss*-ing."

Tiny Tranh taps at the door, peeking around.

"May I come in?" she's almost whispering, "I think I forgot my sunglass."

She finds them quickly beneath her seat and putting them on looks at Dat like a model in an Italian sunglasses ad.

Dat, with great show, sticks his tongue through his teeth. "Sunglass-*izzzzz*," he corrects, but it's a gentle, bemused correction, a detached correction. The sigh he sighs now is pure—infinite light—relief.

"Good!" Larry says and sleep*ssssssssss* well that night for the first time in years.

UN DIVERTISSEMENT

"First you forget names, then you forget faces.
Next you forget to pull your zipper up and finally,
you forget to pull it down." George Burns

M r. Darcy Wolfsie points at the leftmost
of four Currier and Ives lithographs
he's masking-taped to his black board.

"Childhood," he taps the chalk,

Tap

Tap

216

And unbuttons the *second* collar button of his blue Oxford, aping Esdras, a tanned, muscular shaved-head surfer from Puerto Escondido a few rows back.

On the left, "The Season of Joy" depicts four young children collecting buttercups, feeding grass to a baby lamb, cavorting, reclining, contemplating a nosegay of spring flowers. Oblivious…

…then again…?

Another student, Ana, in a tight red tee shirt "oohs," recalling her own season of joy in Bogota.

To its right, "Youth. The Season of Love." It's a wonder the couple strolling hand-in-hand, staring so intently into each other's eyes, doesn't veer off the country path into the wheat field.

Soon Yoo "ahs", and her snug yellow tee shirt rises with the thought of Ji-hun back in Seoul.

Further right, a smiling wife passes her new baby to her mutton chopped, be-spatted husband at the door while three more children and a dog clamor and shout, "Daddy, daddy!" Daddy somehow has the stamina to smile back. Of course. It's "Middle Age. The Season of Strength."

And, Paramaswari "hummms" with the promise of greeting her own Mohan at the door. When her blue tee shirt exposes her lotus jewel navel, Mr. Darcy Wolfsie reddens.

His eyes alternate between her belly button and this lithograph, where he pauses, lingers, dawdles; he identifies with it,

or maybe fears moving on to the next.

Red Ana, yellow Soon Yoo, and blue Parameswari giggle at Mr. Wolfsie suddenly puffing up his blue oxford, sucking in his gut, running his hand around his waist, standing so erect, grinning, flirting? sweeping back some imaginary hair. They giggle along with Esdras, the surfer from Escondido, and Esdras pops open the *third* button of his tight black shirt.

"Season of Strength," he taps the chalk on the board again. "Season of Strength…,"

Tap

Tap

Tap

And the tapping is the nicking of the tri-fin
of

Darcy's

Surfboard over the deadly coral inches below
the surface

His board, small, compact

As maneuverable as

an Alfa Romeo

arms at his sides

Nonchalant, like waiting for a bus

But, one false move and this tsunami,

this Mount Rushmore

this behemoth

219

Moai sculpture

dashes him to bits on the coral right before the

eyes of a phalanx of Pentaxes whirring on tripods

adoring him

before the eyes of a triumvirate of Ray Banned bikinied Billibong babes on shore, one red, one yellow, one blue, running thumbs around bottom seams.

And, to think Marina said, "Too tight. Those jeans make you look…,"

"Ha! My dear Marina. Just look up from your "O" Magazine a moment. You shall see."

And, for Marina, for the three girls who almost resemble a Colombian flag, he carves with the finesse of a man slicing his forty-fifth Thanksgiving turkey, a butcher extraordinaire, down five stories of aquamarine, "Feeding Mother" sea face with yellow clown fish, blue parrots, red napoleons embedded like chunks of pig floating in head cheese.

The clickety clack of his fin is

a sculptor's hammer on chisel

steel wheels on rails

authority made manifest

He toys with the vicious foam ball nipping at
his heels, like the hounds of hell, for *effect,* a
stuntman slaloming past a line of phony bullets.

And the red, yellow, blue flag of bikinis
"oohs" and "ahs" and undulates in the offshore
wind.

His left hand scoops the pocket. He's piped,
tubed. A lesser mortal would be annihilated, swept
clean away as if Potemkin Villages on Bikini Atoll.

But *his* legs are pile-driven stanchions in
bedrock. His body hard as surfboard fiberglass,
taut as an ankle leash stretched near snapping in a
lung-burning wipe out. He's a tanned, Zen spare,
Adonis lifeguard.

A surfing machine. One with the board, the
board one with the wave. Just a mere thought and
it careens where he wishes.

"My god," the girls giggle-whisper, "he almost looks bored."

"Eeeew, way cool," they flourish back three errant strands of blond hair in unison.

He steps back, digs in, pivots to avoid Kelly, the bald ten-time champ just paddling out, spritzing him in the face as he passes.

Mr. Wolfsie shakes the water from his hair and feints a sweeping, sinewy curve,

tempts the wave, dares it to catch him, obliterate him.

"I don't see how he can come back out? Impossible! He'll be crushed by thirty-five tons of water," one commentator opines, covering his blond head with his arms.

"This is gonna be bad. Real bad," proffers his partner, also protecting his head.

The three bikinis avert their eyes and drop their iPhones in the sand.

But he rockets out like a shard of shrapnel, like a shinkansen bullet train

Swoops up in his trademark Immelmann inverted-loop ejection,

somehow hovering at the apex,

defies gravity like Millikan's oil drop experiment, suspended in a shimmery, salty aura, a billion tiny rainbows. The petrels cock their heads in disbelief.

"Way rad," the bikinis yell and search for an invisible wire up to the hovering copter, for surf angel wings, perhaps?

Bald Kelly, bobbing over a huge swell, drops his jaw.

Then

Splash.

A blue plastic pail, a mouthful of sea water.

"Darcy, Darcy, you OK ?" Marina, his wife, screams.

The three bikinis are hovering, fingers at grape glossy lips. "He was on his knees," the red one says.

Marina tosses a Mickey Mouse towel over his hips.

"Costco Wave Storm board. One 'o those foamy toy boards. Mile long." Yellow adds.

"Barely a wave," volunteers Blue, chuckling.

And it's as obvious as the tiny black Speedo beneath the tanned belly, as glaring as the massive golden neck chain of the Italian tourist trying to get a glimpse of Darcy Wolfsie stretched out on the sand. As clear as the eyes of every gawking stroller, every frown, raised eyelid, index finger twisted at a temple.

"Wobbling...," Blue juts her chin at Darcy's blue rash guard hiked up around his massive belly, "like a blubbery whale."

"Red kayak, but he couldn't get outta the way. Bam!" Yellow slaps her palms together. "Thought maybe it was a heart attack."

Bald Kelly, lugs two halves of an enormous geezer surfboard, almost a Duke Kahanomoku koa wood sixteen-footer, and something blue up the beach eliciting chuckles.

When Darcy tries to turn, he winces and creaks like a rusty bicycle bottom bracket. Newton has overridden Archimedes and Darcy can barely sit up.

"Hey old man," bald Kelly calls out.

And for a moment Darcy ignores the voice.

Then the Red Sea of bikinis parts, and grinning bald Kelly proffers Darcy's shredded blue Roxy surf trunks, dangling sprigs of seaweed and tiny bits of white coral.

Darcy, still oblivious, reaches out as if for some surf trophy, eyes wide, lips parted.

"Hey, dude," Kelly whispers, "Saw you out there. Not bad…,"

The bikinis ogle Darcy over their Ray Bans, as if he's a two-page color spread in *Surfer* while Kelly plucks out the last morsels of coral and slimy strands of kelp and helps Wolfsie wriggle into the clammy trunks.

"…not bad at all…," he says,

…before that gnarly wipe out. Hey, old man, get some *rest*."

Darcy Wolfsie *double* knots the short cord on his trunks, then, just enough cord remaining, knots it a third time.

"Mr. Wolfsie? Mr. Wolfsie?" Ana says.

"Mr. Wolfsie, you OK?" Soon Yoo adds.

"Mr. Wolfsie, the pictures, what about the pictures? Middle age? adds Parameswari.

"Oh yes," he clears his throat and taps at "Middle Age. The Season of Strength." "In the US, Middle Age is roughly…well…," and he cocks his thumb back at his own finely-ironed blue shirt, open two buttons at the neck.

The girls eye each other, then Esdras, then Mr. Wolfsie, and the class stirs, protests, rumbles as if Mr. Darcy Wolfsie has tried to tell them to use "if I were" in the subjunctive mood.

All eyes go right, to the last lithograph.

"Uh…Mr. Wolfsie," Parameswari begins, then abandons her thought. In Tamil Nadu they are taught to respect the professor.

By a raging fire, a cat, a granddaughter look up at grandpa reading a newspaper, grandma, knitting. But look closer…they are napping. This is "Old Age. The Season of Rest."

And Mr. Darcy Wolfsie, with some hesitation, buttons his second neck button and taps on the picture.

"IT'S GONNA TAKE AN OCEAN…,"

"When the mind becomes quiescent, the world will disappear." Sri Ramana Maharshi

Mr. Xin Yuan, red Air India slippers, red sleep mask pulled down below soft brown baby spider monkey crew cut and above skittering restless brown eyes naps 35,000 feet above the Atlantic.

228

On his headphones, the news gives him some surcease.

He doesn't really listen, but the drone, the white noise, fills his tortured mind, and shuts it off.

At home, he sleeps with a tiny blue transistor radio and ear phone jammed in his right ear.

"Only way to sleep," he counters when his wife, Jin, scoffs.

He's seen all of the in-flight movies, some twice.

A thin sliver of sunlight penetrates his mask, and Pritti, a red-saree-d flight attendant is bending close. Yuan inhales a heady mixture of garam masala and attar.

"Mr. Xin, Sir, your usual." Pritti brushes close while Yuan lowers his tray table over a Lonely Planet guide to India laid open on his lap to a double-page spread of the priapic Konark sun temple carvings, his bookmark a wallet-sized photo of a ridiculously afro-ed guru grinning in orange robes. The guide is as dog-eared as an Hasidic scholar's *Talmud*, an Imam's *Koran*, a priest's *Bible*, a

Sadhu's *Baghavad Gita*, a monk's *Satipatthāna Sutta*, a Sikh's *Adi Granth*, a Zoroastrian's *Zend-Avesta*.

He samples a fork of palak paneer, but cannot eat, for Pritti has come to life, writhing before him in the brown stone color plates of the book on his lap.

He lays down the fork, plucks out the guru bookmark, stuffs it into the seat pocket, holds his head in his hands and weeps.

"Quiet the mind. Quiet the mind," he mumbles. "So easy for *him* to say." The soulful black eyes of the guru peak out above the seat pocket. Yuan jams the bookmark deeper then cocks his thumb aft.

"So easy for *them* to say." His thumb faces east. "So easy for *all* of them. Damn them!"

"Om," he hums, closing his eyes, trying his best, "Om," he strains.

"Om," teases Pritti with wide shiva-lingam eyes.

"Om, baby! Om!"

230

Egad!

"We'll bury you out back," Jin, his wife, is
fond of joking, "just off my garden, next to Bingo."

And Yuan will laugh, and two plus two will
equal four, why should it not?

But now, *out back,* scythe in hand, the math is
all wrong.

No matter how he slices it: commutative,
distributive, associative, addends, subtrahend,
minuends, multiplicands, left to right, top to
bottom, vice versa, Yuan is getting *five.*

What gives? This thickly tangled green
ground cover spread before him, so lush, so
verdant, almost *begging* to be hacked away, as if for
its own demise.

231

But why? What would it have to gain? A sacrifice for some greater gain? Something up its chlorophylled sleeve? Yuan, too wrapped up in himself, gives it no thought. He's on a mission.

A shame, as we'll discover soon.

"Right about here," Leaning on his scythe, he visualizes a space

not much larger than himself,

sweeps one palm faced upwards, "between these two palms. Perfect."

He has at the quixotic tangle of vines, in bare-chest, cargo shorts, low boots, a sopping scarlet paisley Elephant bandana around his forehead.

Like the droning radio news, the salty sweat, the aching arms and back, the hot sun beating down give him respite. And, he hacks away with abandon. For a moment, a particularly intransigent slithery tangle of roots, curiously resembling Pritti on the Konark Temple, breaks the spell, but, wielding the flattened end of a pickaxe, he obliterates it, spewing black sap everywhere, and in no time gets back to business.

In their death, the bleeding leaves' tiny faces seem to grin as if getting in the last word, as if exacting a final revenge. But Yuan fails to notice. No matter. It's too late now.

Bunches and bunches of tri-lobed green vines he slices, hugs to his chest, stuffs into bag after black plastic bag, their toxic white-to-black sap mingling with his salty sweat, their tiny white berries falling hither and thither, rolling about in the folds and crevices of his skin. Some vines, in one ultimate reprisal, like razors, slice open his skin as if he's some 13th century flagellant monk, and he relishes the momentary abandon.

Judy, his neighbor, eyes him from across her bare slat fence, trying to catch his eye, wagging three fingers, mimicking a stomach-scratching-monkey, but Yuan is blissfully oblivious.

But not for much longer.

By sunset, Arnold Palmer could putt on it. He leans on a well-worn rake handle and lets out a sigh. "I'm ready," he says, "ready to *go home.*"

A nice ring this phrase, spiritual yet prosaic, simple, like getting on the 3:23 to New Haven. "Tomorrow," he muses, "tomorrow, I'll dig."

Is the shiver that flutters through him, like the prodromal tingle on a lip before a herpes eruption, a shiver or a doubt? So faint, as if a drop of iodine in a limpid mountain lake, a single syphilis spirochete in the blood, a lone Lassa fever virus in the lungs.

"Odd," he utters aloud while showering, feeling a tad out of sorts. "Quite odd, indeed." He shakes his head, dismisses the thought.

Within a day, tiny welts are rising, each one an itch machine.

"No-see-ums," dismisses Jin, "you're such a hypochondriac." And she turns back to tend her tomatoes.

Yuan tries to dig in his putting green plot but makes little headway, more scratching than shoveling.

When he abandons the shovel in the garage, his hole is barely big enough for a Beagle.

By the second day, Yuan gives up all hope of digging.

Who can dig slathered with pink lotion? Every square inch of skin save face, hands, and feet. God bless the gloves. Cursed be the ankle socks.

And, ready or not, like it or not,

no choice Buster! Yuan is blindsided, in the fight of his life,

for his life.

He empties several bottles of fuchsia salve before seeking help.

And, the avuncular doctor, eyebrows peaked, confirms it. "Worst case I've seen. You can *die* from this. Good thing you came in when you did."

And Yuan bends over for the shot.

"You'll have a bit of trouble sleeping, maybe, nothing to worry about," the doctor pats him on the shoulder and shows him out.

A greater understatement has never been voiced.

For several weeks, the itch makes him long to jump headlong from the Empire State Building His only strength? That he's not one of those poor souls, not too long ago, who *did* scratch themselves, their pus-oozing sores, to death.

At least *he* has the pills

But the aloe

And benzocaine

And Technu

And bananas

And baking soda

And alcohol

And bleach

And vinegar

And orange juice

are as effective as holding the stick *back* in a graveyard spiral.

He slices the legs off his pants

The sleeves from his shirts

"fuck, fuck, fuck," he intones as Guru Baba Urushiol has directed.

His legs swell.

His head swirls

"I think... I'm dying...,"

The nurse hangs up.

"Wait it out, run its course," they say.

Klondike gold fever, at least, had its paydirt, its gloryhole.

He thinks solely of urushiol.

It's urushiol fever;

It's war!

Eliminate it at all cost!

238

Yet it is no ordinary foe.

It's the wiliest of enemies.

A grizzled guerrilla willing to fight to the death.

Neither scalding shower, nor blow torch, nor sand paper, nor sulfuric acid, nor boiling water would make the slightest dent. It's the Craziest of Crazy Glues, like a bowling ball sticks to an Reckon, a hard hatted man to a crane. After a mere ten minutes it's a fait accompli, as irreversible as an increasing entropy reaction.

Still, he scratches his blistery ankles to bleeding on the shower floor.

The behavior of an insane man?

Perhaps.

But then it goes from bad to worse.

Yuan could be on crystal meth. Through the long night, he scrubs the floor on hands and knees, wanders around the neighborhood nearly naked like a mad man, clothes too painful on skin.

Writhes

atop the bamboo bathroom floor entreating god to put him out of his misery. He'll gladly trade places with those four unfortunate policemen pinned beneath the World Trade Center rubble. At least *they* need not scratch. If he's lucky enough to doze off, he awakens hourly, as if with a critically colicky baby, to scratch, and to lather on the magenta unguent as thick as papier mache, hot blow dry it into a plaster of Paris that barely soothes before cracking into a dry arroyo of fissures.

.

Purplish smears and smudges, flakes of hot pink grainy dust collect everywhere—beds, chairs, rugs, food--over weeks and weeks.

When he finally goes cold turkey, shivering, sweating beneath a pile of twisted blankets in the ER, he longs for the itch, pleasant in comparison.

He looks down upon his thrashing self.

Who am I? he inquires.

"Please let this end!"

And, in bed that same evening, still under his plush brown bear sleeping bag—true, the only thing soft enough to tolerate—he notices his tiny blue transistor has disappeared. He hasn't listened in weeks! Hasn't even thought about it. He's simply forgotten.

He turns to Jin lying beside him, studying a Burpee catalogue.

241

"Honey? Where's my...?"

But stops mid-sentence.

It's a minor miracle.

Then, he turns and falls fast asleep.

The next morning, just after sunrise, he soaps down the scythe, the shovel, the rake.

Dish soap only.

Yellow rubber gloves.

Drenches all with isopropyl alcohol.

Scrubs again with Technu.

Then again.

Tosses the gloves like a nuclear plant worker going off shift, burns the sneakers, ankle socks, shorts, yellow tee shirt, and just to be on the safe side, the white bath towels.

He makes quick work of the Beagle-sized hole and tamps it down with his sneaker. He listens only to the birds, the breeze through the leaves, the buzzing mosquitoes and bees.

A calm suffuses his body as he clap-clap-claps his palms together.

Done.

He dials Air India.

"I'd like to go to Tiruvannamalai," he inquires.

"Yes sir," the woman, her voice quite like Pritti's, says, "absolutely sir. Now, would you like the regular or vegetarian meals?"

THE CLAVICLE

"The physical appearance of temptation becomes
the spiritual recognition of salvation." A Course in
Miracles

Ondina's bright orange scoop-neck blouse
does not befit Father Burgee's vision of
a director of his soup kitchen. It should

be a chaste, well-wrapped Mother Theresa tapping lightly at the door to his study.

"Father Clark?" nor does Ondina's sultry voice match her job. It should have the inflection of a tired schoolmarm explaining quadratic equations by grouping. "I need to ask you, uh Father Clark. We're running short on coffee…,"

"Oh! Mrs. Riley, Mrs. Riley. Didn't see you, sorry, come in, come in."

Father Burgee looks up from his sermon. Ondina has caught him mid-gesticulation, a broad swath, his Brooks Brothers'ed arm carving an arc of judgment, blame, criticism out his window, specifically at that huge *billboard of scantily-clad bimbos cavorting over the strip mall.* Concupiscence personified.

Rev Clark Burgee flattens his tie, a dark tie framed by a dark vest itself framed by a dark pin-stripe suit.

"Yes, yes, coffee, of course. I'll have Jane get on it right away, right away. Anything else? Mrs. Riley. Anything else?"

He has a tendency to repeat himself in direct proportion to his nervousness.

"Ondina, please," she says.

Ondina's blouse repulses him, its shameful bright orange, shameful plunging scoop-neck, coarse, silk-screened pattern of repugnant silver dollar-sized Marilyn Monroe faces alternating right-side-up, up-side-down. So bargain basement, so Beall's Outlet. Pants, too, a shapeless, taste-less, tacky, loose-fitting, orange.

It's the same orangey-red of the Elmo, splayed upon the chair across his desk. Elmo, not five minutes ago, in the tiny hand of his tiny son, Luke. And Luke's tiny hand, five minutes earlier in his mother's, Clark's dear tweed-suited wife, Mathilde "Matty" Burgee.

"Come along, Luke, dear," she'd said half-in, half-out the wainscoted office, "let's leave your daddy in peace. He needs to finish up. Love you dear."

"Love you too,"

Before Clark had noticed the forsaken Elmo, Mrs. Reverend Burgee—Matty--and son, Luke, were climbing in their forest green Volvo.

"Ugly," Clark mutters and pops the cover of his pocket watch with his thumb. He kneads thumb against forefinger, feeling the very clamminess, grit of her polyester blouse. "Tacky, trashy, cheap, chintzy, vulgar." He kneads synonyms, too. "It must…crawl…on the skin…

Her skin

Oh

Her skin so *smooth, like fine China.*

Must irritate.

Must irritate that *lovely skin*

"You must positively break out in a rash?" I'll ask.

What are you thinking? You can't ask, can't ever ask.

And, he's repulsed by his nascent fascination.

247

Wonders from whence ariseth? Why does He send it? And who exactly is He?

But let us call a spade a spade.

"Fascination" is hardly adequate for this sudden onslaught.

This Siren.

"Fascination" barely describes Odysseus, lashed to the mast, stuffing his ears with beeswax.

His august will is no match for the way she pulls back her long, black hair, neatly, primly, orderly, yet not *too* tightly, softly, free;

Captivating.

the way her detestable, disgustingly orangey-red blouse drapes itself,

displaying

framing

riveting his eyes upon her long neck.

drawing them down

To that lovely hollow

Between

The body's only two horizontal bones.

the keys to the lock of a Roman door.

Between Ondina's collar bones, her clavicles

diamonds on black velvet,

he must touch this gap

he's Faust; he'll do anything for a chance, just one chance.

But Elmo, damnable Elmo! She mustn't see him.

Is this, then, his point of no return?

Is this that invisible point beyond which keratosis becomes full-blown weepy melanoma?

[concave to convex?]

Or can Clark still be saved?

249

Is he already a reprobate, a sinner, or must it be in flagrante delecti?

No matter, not right now, anyway, for he must get rid of Elmo. If *she* sees that blasted Elmo, he'll never get his old wrinkled fingers upon her skin: young, taut, porcelain-like, draping silken over that niche between those two clavicles, undulating, as if hand for his glove, key for his lock, substrate for his enzyme, soft lips for his soft lips.

Never rest in the nest at the base of her lovely, long swan neck, that oasis, shelter in that port in the storm, that Balm in Gilead.

So, when Ondina turns, he lunges for Elmo, and kicks him with his black loafer, onto the braided carpet beneath his desk; *does Elmo scream?*

It would seem so, for Ondina turns back prematurely and catches the red flashing glint as he sails under Clark's desk.

But

She

Says

Not

A

Thing.

No,

Rather, she rests two long slender fingers on
Clark's black morocco-bound PhD thesis on
the bookcase

As he would rest his own on that hallowed
space

and she evinces a most convincing interest.
"the…Asian…paradigm…in…the…
Christian…tradition." She sighs a breathy,
Marilyn Monroe gasp. "Ooh…Quite a
mouthful," she's nearly panting. "Do tell…
do tell…,"

Clark, not usually at a loss for words, is speechless save for babbling something about *one god, only one true god..*

Inside, though, he's prolix, as if defending his doctoral thesis, as if questioner and defender simultaneously.

The glen between her clavicles? Why not? A turn of a breast, curve of a hip, pout of a lip, glint of an emerald eye, taper of an index finger, timbre in a voice, accidental brush of arm upon arm, whiff of yesterday's perfume. Anything will do. Why not this beautiful trough?

Ondina, smiling with parted lips, inches toward Rev Burgee, glances down at the swale between her own two clavicles then at Clark as if to say *what's all the fuss about?* With eyes demurely cast down, she radiates innocence; when she stares up at him, it's something again, and Clark is embarrassed.

While she steps around his mahogany desk, Reverend Clark Burgee pictures his bevel-edged lawn,

Three bikes for ornaments

blue stucco,

maple-y cul-de-sac,

his golden Toyota,

Matty's white Minivan

An intense pain in his tingling fingers jolts him.
The agony of deprivation. For that luxurious
velvety valley, that satiny trough between Ondina's
twin silken clavicles—does it have a name?—is
millimeters from his lips and longs to be stroked,
surfed like a warm Tahitian wave, caressed, *my god!*
dug into, palpated, manhandled, ravaged.

His fingers, like Michelangelo carving his Pieta in
his sleep, flex uncontrollably, involuntarily.

And Ondina's green eyes leap from his fingers to
his eyes to his fingers again, signaling, lifting,
guiding, orchestrating, conducting. *How can it be?*

Yet, it's not to be, not this time, for as his fingers close that last micrometer, jockey for final position, for purchase, go in for the kill, as it were, Elmo, just over there, out of the corner of Clark's addled, inflamed eye, intercedes.

"Ahem," Elmo blurts out, and that's all it takes.

A close call.

And "ahem" is what Clark repeats to Ondina—*uh, ahem, Mrs. Reilly*-- and Elmo stares, arms akimbo, not budging, like a kindergarten teacher waiting for Johnny to apologize, until he sees Clark's hand stop. But only when he's seen Clark's arm backtracking, pulling away, does Elmo break his stare, only then does he back down..

*****

Perhaps a close call this time. But, this obsession--we cannot call this love—this obsession, has no cure. This addiction, this melanoma, if you will, will take its ultimate toll, will wreak its ultimate havoc--it may take some time; it can afford to take its time---but that it will do so is as sure as the mortgage on Clark's one-story blue stucco, Clark and Matty's stucco.

There is no known cure.

Or is there?

Well, we get ahead of ourselves.

*****

Some weeks later—the exact time does not really matter—this tiny, innocuous gap betwixt clavicles, this undulation, has worked its magic, insinuated itself, inserted itself, made itself comfortable, made itself at home, *mi casa es su casa*, latched on, rooted, and convinced him (as if he really needed convincing). Clark, to his credit, had protested; vapidly to be sure, mere lip service, crocodile tears. Nothing really newsworthy, for here we are, some weeks later, Clark on a bed, in a room, in a hotel—in fact, in Philadelphia, but it could be anywhere. Next to him is Ondina, but she, too, could be anyone. It's her sternum—is that what it's called?-- he lusts after, but the pieces and parts are interchangeable, one size fits all.

"I didn't know you had an Uncle Bill in Philadelphia?" Matty, his wife was taken aback as she helped him pack.

"Well, actually, it's Uncle Bill from LA."
"LA?"

"Uncle Bill in LA," he repeats. Matty jams a shirt in the corner of his suitcase. "Maybe I never told you? Anyway, heart attack, business trip to Philly. Terrible thing…most terrible thing."

"Oh. Yes, terrible thing."

"Not a moment to lose."

"Well, hurry back. Love you." And Matty had pecked him on the lips.

"I'll try," he'd said, "but you know how these things are, and…,"

"Dad, dad, dad, bring us back something…,"

A trite red silk-sheeted bed at that—slipcover yet unturned—and fluffy, white bathrobes, two glasses of wine, eyes locked and oblivious.

If you, dear reader, have given Clark the benefit of the doubt up to this point, perhaps it's now time to give in. For, they are seconds from crossing that one-way bridge. That bridge that exacts an huge toll. Elmo is thousands of miles distant, and Clark is ready. All lights are green; all systems go. "Bravo, Clark," he even congratulates himself, "you've finally learned to live in the moment, the now. Enlightenment!" But perhaps this is not really the moment they had in mind.

He takes her in, savors her, before the plunge. Anticipation, they say, is ninety percent of the pleasure, and he wants his full portion. Those clavicles, damnit, could hang in the Louvre, hang in museums worldwide, hang, in fact, right now beneath a pearl necklace just across the Schuylkill River outside their window.

Ready, finally, he sets his wine class on the night stand, and starts his hand in the high arc, slow, deliberate, at first, then faster, a voice calling out *hurry, man, hurry*.

At the apex, fingers spread, unfold like the spindly legs of a Lunar Excursion Module, preparing for touchdown, smooth landing, like the "Super Catcher" claw machine game, grabbing for the fuzzy dice, ready to engulf as much as he can in one fell swoop…

Perhaps it's the first rays of a Philly sunrise angling in through the window, perhaps the wine fog, perhaps the fine, silken, glittery dust of powder, the light golden bronze, perhaps her gulp, her nervous swallow that causes her throat to flutter. And that hollow in her clavicle is as lovely and inviting as an Irish village nestled between two lush green hills.

Yet so was Matty's once, too.

He recalls the moment he first touched it

Kissed it

He'd thought of Modigliani

A red necklace

And, his hand pauses in midair

But not to worry

Only a momentary

holding pattern

Burn off some fuel

Wait for the weather to clear

He's committed to land

As if an autopilot capturing the glide slope

He's locked in

His eyes have latched on to, honed in on that
juncture between Ondina's clavicles

But an odd thing transpires.

He falls, as it were, into that hollow, almost a
chasm, this gorge, this ravine, this cleft, this furrow,
this fissure, almost a crevasse, joining her two
horizontal bones, cet "Genou de Claire"

So deep,

Penetrating, probing, thrusting, so
powerfully, with such abandon, that he goes not
only to the hilt, the cervix, but then deeper than
deep, below below, beneath beneath,

he implodes

Jake LaMotta whipped to a frenzy

His whole body subsumed by her silken skin

Looks out of her radiant jade eyes

Feels himself as her luscious pomegranate and rose bliss body vagina

As her satiny thighs

As her pendulous pear-like breasts being suckled by himself

He's inside-out.

But then deeper still,

Subtle body upon subtle body

the s, p, d, and f orbitals of the atoms of his skin

intermingle

Intercalate

With hers

And it's a covalent sigma bond fuck

A fuck with more names than god.

Periodic table of fuck.

Quantum copulation.

261

Tantric fuck more fantastic than the
"Voyage."

He's Shakti; she Shiva

Yin-yang

Sun-moon

Yamuna-Ganges

God-goddess

Ridiculous?

But, for a brief instant

   An *holy* instant

   He catches a glimpse of

   That which *is* eyes, vagina, breast, thigh, and
clavicles

   Of *That which created them*

   And all that preceded

   And which preceded that

As infinitum

reductio ad absurdum

And

Miracle of miracles

The pain, the agony of denial

The melanoma of obsession-beyond-cure

The weepy, seepy, vaginal, pudendal carcinoma

Flares, one last time, frighteningly,
threateningly, Custer's last stand, fight to the finish,
death match, it shan't go easily into the night

Clark's fingers are still an Angstrom distant; so
close that inter-molecular forces kick in, dipole to
dipole

It flares

Spectacular

White hot

annealing

like an exploding

Dying

Supernova

He's ejected

Thrown out

Rocketed into the stratosphere

Then it

Flickers

And

Is

Is

Is

But it takes a bit of time

It is not an easy thing

This dying ember seems to go on forever

But is

At long last

Gone.

Ondina--Clark gazes at her--is now not exactly *beautiful*

Well, yes, she *is* beautiful

But, she is beautiful

In a strange new way

beautiful

Because *She with a capital s* is beautiful

He squeezes her hand

An unusually

Loving squeeze

A Namaste squeeze

And he smiles

but even still a drop-of-India-ink-in-a-mountain-lake hint of disappointment mixed with his contentment

Spent and calm,

He trades fluffy white bathrobe for chinos,

Pads over to the window and calls Matty

"The strangest thing just happened," he tells her.

"Yes, I was having a dream," He's woken Matty from a deep slumber.

"Oh?"

"Your uncle?"

"He…he…he…passed," Clark says.

"I'm sorry."
"He's in a better place," he says.

"True," she says, "He *is* in a better place."

Ondina brushes back her perfect silken black hair with perfectly beautiful slender fingers, smiles perfectly, eyes glint perfectly, breasts undulate perfectly, the curve of her neck, her arm, all ballet perfect. Who can argue? How perfect indeed.

"I really must be going," says Clark, turning at the door to wave.

His eyes fall upon a small strand of Ondina's hair that's popped out of its tie, and drapes itself across her forehead. It glows in the light, stands out from the other hairs, calling attention to itself. Who can explain? The synergy of shock of hair on forehead. This coquettish lock dangles, bobs down to the eyelash, undulates, beckoning, playing, teasing him.

But how tawdry, how repulsive, how unkempt, how casual, how disorderly.

She's divine!

"Tawdry," he says, now aloud. "Yes, tawdry," he repeats, "How tawdry, indeed. I really must be going. Must be going."

And Ondina brushes the little shock of hair up off her forehead, but the unruly tress plummets down again; she brushes again, and Clark's hand twitches and moves of its own accord.

ADOLFO, THAT VISIGOTH

"We must learn to regard people less in the light of what they do or omit to do, and more in the light of what they suffer." Dietrich Bonhoeffer

"Champagne," Adolfo raises a glass, and grins a puffy grin at his own cleverness, "like drinking stars."

A collective groan, as redolent as the mole sauce on the bacalao, wafts up and over the blond wood dinner table.

With thick, soft-from-turning-too-many-pages fingers, Adolfo rakes back greasy brown, shoulder-scraping Visigoth hair, then strokes scraggly, salt-pepper beard.

"You *must* grill the peppers," he regales, gripping an imaginary lectern. Then shovels a tortilla chip into his slimy lips, *"mwahs"* his bunched fingertips, and downs a shot of Courvoisier with a Burt Lancaster grimace.

"One doesn't really *drink* it," he brandishes the snifter at arm's length, "as much as *savor* it, then swishes, sniffs, gulps again.

My daughter—his niece--Tillie, takes it all in behind thick, tweeny glasses, daring glances up from her salad, as if a Mann in audience with Fuehrer. Looks up at her uncle, Adolfo, as if he's the Dylan on her black tee-shirt. Or at least as if he'd been there,

Folk City,

Bleecker Street

Greenwich Village

Wow!

Her salad scatters across the table, and not saying anything, she collects a cucumber slice here, plum tomato there, black olive, shard of escarole, leaf of arugula, heart of romaine with chubby, awkward fingers.

Her eyes roll inward behind those thick black glasses, part embarrassed, but mostly New York City swoon. Adolfo misses the embarrassment; it's something only a mother might detect.

Then Adolfo's eyes--reddish-green--roll back, his for a different reason. And thank god! He's on the verge of listing, ready to topple, capsize. If I can hold out a tad more, he'll do himself in. The mole, green tomatillo, chopped onions, shitake mashed potatoes will rival Diego Rivera on the placket of his yellow habanera, on his pasty, wan, Big Apple face.

He grows quiet--maybe someone'll get a word in edgewise—and then, for a brief instant, his faraway red eyes betray a nuance, a tinge of longing, disappointment perhaps?

Is it our hopelessly un-hip, "Little Apple", Steinberg's west of Ninth Avenue, west-of-the-Hudson sensibility?

271

Tillie, re-constructing her salad, misses it.

But then he downs another shot with a teeth-baring grimace, finds his legs, and turns *nasty*. His poor brother, Franciso, immaculately tidy pony tail, tries to re-insert the bloated cork in the Courvoisier and takes the brunt of it.

"They were this big," Adolfo balls his fists like huge hailstones, knuckling his brother on the head, "those damned things could hurt you."

Francisco, tries to fend him off with raised palms.

"Wimped out on me," Adolfo glowers, "Left him under a goddamned pine tree while I went up to the top."

"B-b-b-but I couldn't *breathe*," Francisco grabs his asthmatic throat with one hand, the other blaming the picante sauce for his tears.

"And he calls himself a *runner*. Ha!"

Tillie's confused eyes ask, *"What's wrong with Uncle Adolfo?"*

Don't worry, Tillie, I love you," mine reply.

"Dessert! Anyone want dessert?"

But Adolfo seems to get angrier. He's indomitable, a modern-day Rasputin. He raises his glass, dappling his leathery face reddish-golden, eyes impossibly vibrant crimson.

"New York!" he counters, leaning forward, sighs at <u>me</u> now, his greasy hair framing his pulpy face. "New York skyline. I 'spose *you've* never seen it drunk, have you? Every thirteen year old New Yorker's done that! But you…," He looks down his bulbous nose, palms my Mexican peasant dress, my twin braids to confirm.

I motion rapid fire to Franciso.

Stop him!

to Tillie

Your daughter!

back to Francisco

For godsake!

General Staffenberg, the briefcase!

Of course! The blue platter with a dozen cannoli laid out like sticks of TNT.

"Dessert!"

"Cannoli," Adolfo drips, oozes sarcasm like the overstuffled pastries.

"From Veniero's. Y'know. Veniero's on East Eleventh."

But, we're Cretins, retards, apostates, Martians.

But, but…didn't we once live so close to Veniero's that the clunk of dishes, aroma of espresso fill our meager, slanting apartment? When *he* was but an urchin in knickers selling bootleg Bob Dylan eight-tracks on the Plaza Garabaldi.

Tillie and her uncle, Adolfo, stare up at Veniero's hammered copper ceiling, and her mouth drops, paralyzed by the infinite spread of pastries before her.

The platter of decadence.

"Every thirteen-year-old," Adolfo's as tenacious as a rabid Quintana Roo monkey with his fangs in a poor tourist's calf, "every thirteen-year-old *New York kid.*"

Tillie is Trilby to his Svengali, and he relishes it.

He steadies himself, right hand against the table-edge lectern, now waving an imaginary laser pointer in his left hand.

"My kids," he says, "*my* kids especially."

And tears well up in his carmine eyes, almost lost amidst the sweat, spittle, salsa on his face?

"Mmm," he rolls his read backwards with a mouthful of cannoli to show how it's done, educate the hayseeds, the rubes, the hicks, "you gotta get out if you wanna be a *writer*. Gotta experience the world."

And Tillie mimics, biting, then rolling her head backwards at exactly the same angle. "Mmm," she echoes.

"Mmm," I say, but I've grown used to the ones at Publix; not bad, and so much simpler.

"Gotta experience things, like my thirteen-year-olds...and...,"

Okay.

Enough.

He's pressed a button.

Gone over the top.

No more!

"Uh, look, Adolfo, it's getting late, early day tomorrow, Tillie's got homework, and...,"

Adolfo glances at his watch.

"But mom, it's only…," Tillie says.

I thrust "Modern Bio" into her hands, spin her shoulders towards her room.

"Exactly!" Adolfo shouts, slams his fist on the table, and the yellow plates jump then crash. "Exactamente! In *New York*"—*New York,* hes Anne Sullivan to Helen, nearly screaming as if directing a language deficient tourist to Lincoln Center—"in *New York*, they're just getting underway; evening's young. My kids, even my thirteen-year kids stay up later than you guys."

Kids.

That's it.

It's the way he says it.

Scripted, practiced—*thirty years* of practice—empty,

canned

like a soap opera doctor giving the bad news one too many times.

A teacher might say it this way.

More a *definition* than anything.

A footnote at the bottom of a page.

And so, just like that, Colonel Brandt has inadvertently slid the briefcase behind the leg of a table. Nay, slid it right out of the conference room altogether.

"Okay, okay. One more cannoli. They really are delicious." I lie

Tillie turns; looks at "Modern Bio", at the cannoli. "But mom, you said...," but I motion her back to the table.

"Your Uncle Adolfo did bring them *all* the way from *New York,* and they aren't getting any fresher."

"But mom...,"

"There are still a *few* things I miss from the City," I'm pouring it on thick. "As long as someone makes more coffee."

"Brought just the thing." Adolfo hands me a blue pound bag of Lavazza espresso. "Can't get coffee like *this* down here."

"No, I 'spose not," I exaggerate, pulling apart the foil and sniffing as if I'm auditioning for a coffee commercial.

And Adolf looks relieved. Relieved to stave off that stack of paragraphs he's brought along to grade, those paragraphs by his *kids,* his thirteen-year-old kids.

"Say," he asks, "maybe tomorrow we can go kayaking. Really enjoy that. Not something you can really do in Central Park, if you know what I mean?

"No, I 'spose not."

Uncle Adolfo passes out on the sofa, and Tillie puts the blue bag of coffee next to another five identical bags on the shelf.

"Mom...? she asks.

THE GATE

"Gate, gate, paragate." from The Heart Sutra

"Dail. Dail. Now, one with the gate open," calls out Leocadia, the lithe, young blond photographer in a white blouse. She's from "Luxury Southern Living" and bends under the weight of a half dozen cameras and black bags. "Now, gate closed. Good."

She's Kovacs; I'm Nicholson.

She's Zigmund; I'm DeNiro.

281

My constituents, er, neighbors, form a semicircle of Talbots and Land's End pastels and leather enclosed by an herd of earth tone Escalades, Range Rovers, Navigators, and Land Cruisers on the grass median, like Pioneers by their Conestoga wagons.

"Now, stand in the center."

She wants the polished granite palm motif middle panel… I oblige, swatting a mosquito on my bare arm.

Splat!

the Mighty Mule dual action motor.

Now, my neck.

Splat.

Snip!

The blue ribbon flutters to the asphalt.

Pressing of flesh.

Applause.

Just outside the gate, a phalanx of Wetba…er…
Mexicans tossing sod in the blistering heat of the
full sun, looks up, wipes sweat with red and blue
bandanas, then resumes tossing.

I grasp a vertical wrought iron bar in each hand
and peer back at them through *my* gate—mine, all
mine, from blueprint to…this.

So solid.

So secure.

Barely a rattle when I shake the bars.

With this baby, hell. They'll never get in. Who needs
ADT?

"Okay, Dail." Leocadia sings out, sweeping
back her blond hair before aiming her Pentax, "one
more with the wife." And Dariana, my raven-
haired better half flicks a mosquito off the shoulder
of my pink shirt, hands me a plastic glass of
champagne, then nuzzles under my left arm. "*Into*
the camera, Mrs. R." Leocadia chastises her. "Into
the camera, please."

For Dariana is eyeing that bum—how else to say it?—that bum, Jay: Yankees cap riding atop a Brillo pad of hair, purple NYU sleeve-less sweatshirt, weedy beard, stogie. Jay Bronicks fighting me from the get-go, nearly scuttled me, almost rained on my parade, spoiled my glory, my moment in the sun.

"In New York," he'd insist, "we don't use gates."

"Whaddya mean you don't use gates? I've seen pictures. You're gated up the wazoo, triple-locks, police bars, iron plates, steel doors," I'd said.

"Up the wazoo." He'd puffed his stogie, a cabbie waiting for a fare. "I like that. No, the neighborhoods, numb nuts. The neighborhoods. In the Big Apple, we rub elbows, sit on the goddamned stoop, all walk on the same sidewalk. The hoi polloi. No one is too goddamned good for anyone else, and…,"

"And, well, why don't you just go back to where you came from…,"

"Well, I just might except I…,"

"Except what?"

"Except…," he'd puffed on his stogie again, "except wouldn't you like to know."

"Honey," I whisper, "the camera. Look into the camera."

Jay sticks his tongue at me. I ball my fist up at him, and Leocadia snaps. Then Jay climbs into his antique maroon Mercedes with the "I Heart New York" and Yankees—bat, ball, top hat--bumper stickers, leaving a wake of burning oil and rumbling muffler.

"You'll be in the May *ish*," Leocadia trills, "Send you a dozen." I slap at a high pitched whine in my left ear.

"Let's get the hell outta here," I grab Dariana's arm, and we race to the black Escalade for refuge.

Doors slam.

AC kicks in.

Then

Two long-haired punks roll up on kayak-sized skateboards just outside the gate, dismount, size up the gate, *my* gate, for a few beats, through the gate at me, then run their boards across the bars like convicts their dinner plates.

But, barely a sound. They gape, dumbfounded. Bars solid as the granite columns. I've acquitted myself well. They try the double-locked bars of the *walk through*, its columns granite and palm filigree too.

They shake.

Nothing.

Fake out! Hah! Safe from the likes of them. They'll never get in. The moat is secure; the castle, my daughter Georgette withing, safe from the hordes. Just as advertised.

The kids mutter to each other; the one in the black work shirt--red-piped oval "Daryl" over his heart—kicks the gate with his sneaker, sweeps back his scraggly mass of blond dreds, and gives me the finger.

"'F' you, too," I scream.

"Dear!?" Dariana grabs my arm as a Pipiens' proboscis penetrates my pinky.

"'F'in mosquito," I slap.

But the Escalade assuages, its ice-cold air, Beethoven, gold-plate factory tint, and shocks smooth enough to allow diamond-splitting, all conspire. It's a soundless, secure, cocoon *within* the cocoon. I angle back the seat, stretch out, barely touching the wheel. I've acquitted myself well, indeed. My father would be proud of me.

Beyonce.

Is this Beyonce?

Dariana's flipped on Beyonce and is gyrating, squirming-grooving to the rhythm.

I reach for the knob, but she blocks my hand.

"You and that…Leo…Leo…?

"Leocadia," I say.

"Leocadia…right…Leocadia from 'Luxury Southern Living'." She glowers at me. "You and that Leocadia were pretty damned chummy back there, don't you think?"

"That's crazy. Hell, look who's talking. Christ, the way you were eyeing that…that…Jay Bronicks. Someone might get the idea…," I say.

But, she cranks up the stereo, blotting me out.

"Y'know." I shout. "Y'know, why would a guy like that come around? I mean he's been doggin' me from the start. I'm his goddamned cause célèbre. Like the QE2 changing course at full steam." I scratch my head.

Dariana turns to look out the window, brushes invisible hairs off her forehead.

"Can't understand. Maybe he just saw the light. Finally *got* the way we do things down here?"

Dariana clears her throat, leans forward reaching out for the stereo.

"Musta just seen it my way, come around. How else t'explain?"

And the tips of Dariana's ears go scarlet, and she brushes more invisible hairs off her forehead, frantic now, as if sweeping away a cloud of anopheles.

She cranks the volume up until the tinted windows are rattling..

"Since when have you liked…," I point at the stereo and screw up my face like I've taken a bite of kimchi.

"Well…uh…he…f'ing…likes it."

"What? Whatdya say?"

"I said *he* likes it."

"Who? What?" I say.

"He likes it," she sighs, and her shoulders straighten.

But, just then, our daughter, Georgette, on the back of Daryl's skateboard, her arms around his skinny waist, her black ponytail unraveling scrunchy at the end, flapping, intertwining with his blond hair flying in the wind, rolls by.

"Hey," I screech around the next U-turn, "that's Georgette!" I roll down the window. "Hey, what the hell's goin' on?"

"Nuthin'," they yell out in unison. "Nothin' old man."

I floor it, and the Escalade fishtails, and I gain on them.

A mosquito bites my ankle, I reach down to splat, and when I look up, they're slipping though the polished granite palm walk through, letting it slam behind them, cackling and both half-raised flipping their birds, twirling them like the eddied wakes of a speedboat.

"Damnit! Damnit to hell." I wave and jab the remote at one of the polished granite columns like Gustavo Dudamel conducting the Simon Bolivar.

And the massive, triple-reinforced, wrought iron gate grinds, grates, slips, flaps slowly

    back and forth,

    an inch open then closed,

    open then closed

    open, closed.

Finally, a tortured, Rodin-dying-in-the-streets-of-Tokyo groan, a puff of electric smoke oddly reminiscent of Jay's cheap stogie, and then…,

    Silence,

Motionlessness.

I climb out of the Escalade, hurl the remote at the gate, which only thuds—muffled, solid, secure, mocking—then I grab a wrought iron bar in each hand and shake.

But, nothing.

I'm sapped, weak and sweating, as if I'm coming down with Yellow Fever.

And the Mexican sod tossers, still going strong, pause to nudge each other with dirty, long-sleeved elbows. They eye me, the gate, giggling and pointing.

For I've fallen to my knees, spent, in the receding whirr of urethane skateboard wheels upon smooth pavement, the fading image of Georgette, her ponytail now unfurled, her black hair now flowing free in the wind.. A good thing, perhaps; my mind is fevered; I might have…,"

Too weak to drive, I let Dariana drive back home. She's rolled down her window.

"I just can't get over it? I mean why would Jay so suddenly…?" I whisper, almost incoherent.

"You say something, Dail? Dear?" Dariana's face—she looks quite beautiful in profile, turned toward the window. The air is a mix of orange blossom, Mercedes exhaust, and the ozone of electrical short circuit—plus a note of rotgut stogie. Dariana inhales deeply, sucking it in.

She shakes her head, distractedly. "You say something dear? Dear? You don't look at all well, Dail, honey."

And another damned mosquito gets me on the elbow.

ABOUT THE AUTHOR

Matthew Treya derives his name from the Sanskrit. He is a husband, father, and English as Second Language teacher in the United States. He enjoys animation and has been writing for as long as he can remember, which is a long time.

63322729R00165

Made in the USA
Charleston, SC
30 October 2016